Elizabeth
Shepard

PENGUIN BOOKS

PENGUIN BOOKS
Published by the Penguin Group
Penguin Books USA Inc., 375 Hudson Street, New York, New York 10014, U.S.A.
Penguin Books Ltd, 27 Wrights Lane, London W8 5TZ, England
Penguin Books Australia Ltd, Ringwood, Victoria, Australia
Penguin Books Canada Ltd, 10 Alcorn Avenue, Toronto, Ontario, Canada M4V 3B2
Penguin Books (N.Z.) Ltd, 182–190 Wairau Road, Auckland 10, New Zealand

Penguin Books Ltd, Registered Offices: Harmondsworth, Middlesex, England

First published in the United States of America by Viking Penguin,
a division of Penguin Books USA Inc., 1995
Published in Penguin Books 1996

1   3   5   7   9   10   8   6   4   2

PUBLISHER'S NOTE
This is a work of fiction. Names, characters, places, and incidents either are the product of the author's
imagination or are used fictitiously, and any resemblance to actual persons,
living or dead, events, or locales is entirely coincidental.

THE LIBRARY OF CONGRESS HAS CATALOGUED THE HARDCOVER AS FOLLOWS:
Shepard, Elizabeth.
H/Elizabeth Shepard.
p.   cm.
ISBN 0-670-85927-3 (hc.)
ISBN 0 14 02.4389 5 (pbk.)
1. Mentally ill children—United States—Fiction.   2. Mothers and sons—United States—Fiction.   3.
Campus—United States—Fiction.   4. Boys—United States—Fiction.   I. Title.
PS3569.H393834H2   1995
813'.54 dc20   94-29464

Printed in the United States of America

Praise for *H*

"Elizabeth Shepard's *H* is an intriguing and often poignant first novel. Shepard renders the world of a twelve-year-old boy with profound psychological problems in such a way that we feel his pain and strength simultaneously."
—Rosellen Brown, *The Women's Review of Books*

"*H* is for *H*ats off! Elizabeth Shepard makes an auspicious literary debut in *H*—an epistolary novel with a memorable protagonist. Benjamin is a haunting and haunted amalgam of *Rain Man* and *The Catcher in the Rye*."
—Anne Edwards

"An enigmatic tribute to individualism, as well as a look at the horror of mental illness and the sadness of isolation. Funny, tearjerking, profound, *H* will work its way into your heart."
—*Boston Herald*

"*H* is a heart-wrenching epistolary novel written with great savvy, severe charm and compassion. The character of Benjamin is as haunting and memorable as any I've read in a long time. I'll want to read everything Elizabeth Shepard writes—and right away!"
—Howard Norman, author of *The Bird Artist*

"Elizabeth Shepard's first novel is both tough and tender, with that special something that marks her as a writer to watch."
—*The Dallas Morning News*

PENGUIN BOOKS

H

Elizabeth Shepard writes and teaches in New York City. She received her Master of Fine Arts degree in writing from Columbia University.

. . . now when I'm writing it's already tomorrow and I'm afraid of getting to the end of yesterday. As long as I go on writing, yesterday is today and we are still together.

— GRAHAM GREENE
The End of the Affair

PART
ONE

LAWRENCE S. DYSAN, M.D.
241 CENTRAL PARK WEST
NEW YORK, NEW YORK 10024
(212) 934-2424

June 5, 1994

Mr. and Mrs. Harold Reston
Directors
Camp Onianta
Bear Mountain Road
Fairfield, New Hampshire 03766

Dear Mr. and Mrs. Reston,

I write this letter with some hesitation, yet I feel it important to introduce you to Benjamin Sherman with words of expertise before you commence a summer with him. He is very much looking forward to camp and I expect he will have a most rewarding experience under your supervision. However, there are a few matters which concern me about Benjamin's enrollment in summer camp, and it is important for you to be aware of his psychological diagnoses and the behavioral symptoms which accompany them.

Benjamin is a contemplative twelve-year-old. His silence makes him appear wise, but his actions reveal a gap between his actual and developmental ages. Benjamin suffers from emotional disabilities which surpass those of typical adjustment disorders. Benjamin exhibits the behavioral characteristics associated somewhat with autism and predominantly with clinical depression. His symptoms can impair his ability to function on an ordinary day. He is not treated with any medication at this time, although I will reassess the possibility of drug therapy in the fall.

The visible degree of his illness can range from barely noticeable to severe. His symptoms can occasionally become extreme. Benjamin has a tendency to become completely engrossed in his fantasy world and will respond to interruptions with a violent temper. He is extremely withdrawn and spends much of his waking hours within the realm of his fantasy. Benjamin is often out of touch with reality insofar as he refuses to concentrate on the matters at hand and resorts to the world of his imagination.

Although he rarely erupts in outbursts characteristic of autism, he is noticeably depressed—he has difficulty sleeping, he eats infrequently, he seems listless and hopeless and silent. He relies disproportionately on his fantasy life—the private realm of his imagination, which is free from outside interference.

The physical focus of Benjamin's fantasy is a stuffed toy in the shape of the letter H, which he carries with him at all times. This "creature," whom Benjamin calls Elliot, is not the source but rather the object of this imaginary arena upon which Benjamin so heavily relies. Whereas it is common for normal children to grow attached to an imaginary friend, Benjamin's relationship with Elliot is atypical and a noticeable mark of his illness. I am concerned about Benjamin's inability to perform without the physical rendition of his fantasy. Benjamin and I have spoken about Elliot's role at camp, and I suggested that he leave his "friend" at home for the summer. I don't foresee this occurring immediately, but it would be wise to encourage Benjamin to send Elliot home.

In spite of my concerns, I do feel that Benjamin is capable of attending camp this summer. I hope that a communal living situation will promote his social skills by enabling him to communicate with his peers. I also expect that he will excel in some creative group activity, perhaps art or music. It is unfortunate, though too common, that Benjamin will be made fun of, that he will be perceived as unusual rather than unique, but children usually move on to new targets rather quickly. Bear in mind that he may be particularly sensitive.

I hope that your 1994 season runs smoothly. Do not hesitate to call if something concerns you or if you have any questions. I will be on vacation for the month of August, but my partner is familiar with Benjamin's case and will be able to assist you. I look forward to hearing the heartwarming stories Benjamin is sure to tell when he resumes treatment in September.

Sincerely,

Lawrence Dysan

Peggy and Jeffrey Sherman
118 Church Street
Middletown, Connecticut 06457

June 12, 1994

Harold and Lucy Reston
Camp Onianta
Bear Mountain Road
Fairfield, New Hampshire 03766

Dear Harold and Lucy,

Benjamin is prepared for camp. His trunk should arrive a few days after you receive this letter, and Peggy will bring him to the bus promptly at 8:00, June 29.

I feel it is necessary to tell you about Benjamin in my own words, since he has very little of his own. Benjamin is a quiet boy and likes to be left alone. He seems content to keep himself busy, just as he is content remaining idle. Benjamin is not a bad kid, he may turn out to be a fine man someday, who can tell, but he is not lively or engaging as so many young boys are at his age. He is not the pitcher on the Little League or the envy of his classmates, if you know what I mean.

Benjamin is generally unsociable. I hope it is a phase that will soon pass. But it is clear to me that Benjamin is a loner and will probably be so into his adult life. Peggy and I have been working with a reputable psychoanalyst in New York, who has made some progress, but the breakthroughs are slow. My wife is quite concerned about Benjamin and has reservations about sending him away. I am only concerned that he will not perform well in a perpetual social situation.

Benjamin is happiest when left alone. We do not press him to speak a great deal, since he has nothing to say, and we hope you will do the same. We hope that Benjamin will learn new skills in athletics, particularly softball and swimming. We will be visiting camp the weekend of July 30. We will bring our own lunch.

Best wishes for a successful season.

Sincerely,

Jeffrey Sherman

Camp Onianta
Bear Mountain Road
Fairfield, New Hampshire 03766
(603) 339-4109

Harold and Lucy Reston, Directors

June 13, 1994

Dear Parents,

It's hard to believe the summer is almost here. We have been working hard with our maintenance staff to set up camp. The tennis courts have been rolled and the lake is almost full, and the hay is being lifted into the barn for the horses to eat. We have purchased some new tools for the shop and a pottery wheel for ceramics. The staff seems like a terrific bunch—energetic and multitalented, with a lot of interest in music.

We have enclosed a short questionnaire, which we would like you to fill out. The questions have to do with your child's general behavior and what changes we should be alerted to. This helps us know your child's habits, interests, and signs of when he's feeling troubled. Please return this form along with an immunization record no later than June 23.

Camp dates, as I am sure you know, are different this year. Our season will run from June 29 until August 24. If possible, please arrange to visit your child sometime in the middle. We will provide a picnic lunch if we know the date of your arrival in advance. If you have any questions or concerns, do not hesitate to call us. We will be in New York as of June 25 in order to ride up on the bus with the children. We will be staying at the Mariott Hotel and can be reached in New Hampshire until then.

Best wishes,

Harold and Lucy Reston

Child's Name:

Date of Birth:

Does your child have any siblings? If so, how do they usually get along?

Are your child's grandparents alive?

Favorite activities in school:

Shunned activities:

Hobbies, interests, etc.:

Things your child hopes to accomplish at camp:

What topics or surroundings make your child nervous or anxious?

How does your child behave when s/he is afraid?

How does your child behave when s/he is tired?

What signals does your child exhibit when s/he is unhappy?

Other comments:

June 19, 1994

Harold and Lucy Reston
Camp Onianta
Bear Mountain Road
Fairfield, New Hampshire 03766

Dear Harold and Lucy,

Our letters must have crossed paths. Your questionnaire
arrived yesterday, and Jeffrey recently sent you a brief note
about Benjamin which stated our major concerns. In any event,
we are sending you a complete response to the questions you
enclosed and hope our insight can be of some assistance.

I assume that Benjamin's trunk has arrived and that his
belongings are intact. Of course in all our hurry we forgot to
pack some important items, and we will send them with
Benjamin on the bus. Would it be possible to load his bicycle on
the bus as well? We don't anticipate that will be a problem, but
please let us know if we need to make other arrangements.

I hope the remaining days of preparation run smoothly.

Yours truly,

Peggy Sherman

Child's Name: *Benjamin Sherman*

Date of Birth: *March 14, 1982*

Does your child have any siblings? If so, how do they usually get along? *Benjamin has a younger sister named Hannah. They don't fight—Benjamin never fights—but they don't play together either.*

Are your child's grandparents alive? *Both of his grandparents are alive on his father's side and his mother's mother is also alive.*

Favorite activities in school: *Spelling, social studies, art.*

Shunned activities: *Drama, gym.*

Hobbies, interests, etc. *Benjamin likes to play with small objects he finds on the floor. He likes building things with his hands and he likes his stuffed toys.*

Things your child hopes to accomplish at camp: *Tennis lessons, softball, riding. Benjamin hopes to get his Red Cross card in swimming.*

What topics or surroundings make your child nervous or anxious? *Large groups of people, mostly. Benjamin is not an anxious or nervous child.*

How does your child behave when s/he is afraid? *Benjamin is not a fearful child either.*

How does your child behave when s/he is tired?
It is difficult to tell when Benjamin is tired. He becomes even more withdrawn.
What signals does your child exhibit when s/he is unhappy? *Benjamin is discontented in silence.*

Other comments: *Please see attached note.*

It is painful for me to write about Benjamin at great length. He is a young boy with a good heart and a mind that seems to get in the way. Benjamin is not dangerous, but he is often unpredictable. One minute he's quiet and self-absorbed, the next he's angry and upset, and we cannot keep track of the transitions that must occur within him to make him change so.

When Benjamin was a toddler we noticed some odd characteristics. He was a baby with jumping, searching eyes one minute and cold, dead ones the next. We tried desperately to make him laugh, but we could not. Then, out of nowhere, he would burst out in a fit of laughter, then coo to himself softly until the private humor ceased. It is difficult for a parent to concede that her child needs help and is unusual. Benjamin does not have many friends, and the children in his class make fun of him. He is extremely small and thin and looks several years younger than he actually is. We have noticed some improvement after a year's work with Dr. Dysan (his title and phone number are listed on Benjamin's health form). But the improvements are slow indeed. Benjamin will not be any problem at camp—he is not disruptive and he commands little attention, and he is able to keep himself busy and satisfied without being entertained. I hope that Benjamin will take risks and learn some new skills—try some new activities like tennis and horseback riding—something that will make him feel good about himself. I'm sure you will find Jeffrey's letter more specific and less emotional than mine tend to be.

Yours truly,

Peggy Sherman

Camp Onianta
Bear Mountain Road
Fairfield, New Hampshire 03766
(603) 339-4109

Harold and Lucy Reston, Directors

June 22, 1994

Dr. Lawrence Dysan
241 Central Park West
New York, New York 10024

Dear Dr. Dysan,
   Thank you for your letter about Benjamin. We are not concerned that he will be a problem at Onianta, and we will, of course, deal with him as we do with every child. Be assured that each camper receives personal attention in order to enhance his strengths and feel comfortable with his weaknesses, and Benjamin will not be treated in an unusual manner simply because he has a disability. The information you provided will remain private, and although it is useful, we have decided not to inform his counselors about either his expected behavior or his diagnosis. Let him be as he feels comfortable. We will try not to curb any of his choices.
   We appreciate your concern, and look forward to meeting Benjamin ourselves.

Best wishes,

Harold and Lucy Reston

16

From the Desk of Peggy Sherman

June 25, 1994

Dear Benjamin,

I hope this letter gets to camp before you do. Daddy and I wanted you to get a letter from us on your first day. I hope the bus ride was fun and that you've met some nice people. Were any of the boys in your bunk near you on the bus? Did you get a good bed next to someone you like? What are your counselors like?

Daddy and I are sure that you will have a wonderful summer at Onianta. We miss you already and will call you on Sundays, and we'll be coming up to visit halfway through the summer.

I Love You!

Mommy and Daddy

Camp Onianta
Bear Mountain Road
Fairfield, New Hampshire 03766
(603) 339-4109

Harold and Lucy Reston, Directors

June 29, 1994

Dear Parents,
  Just a quick note to reassure you that the buses arrived safely and the children are settled in their cabins. Naturally, there were spilled sodas and hair stuck together with bubble gum, but the nurse has given each child a shower, a lice check, and a stamp of approval. We asked the children to write you a postcard right after supper, and we try to keep them writing home twice a week, so you should be hearing from them very soon.
  Of course it rained when the buses pulled in and hasn't stopped since. Already the laundry bags are filled with wet socks, and muddy shoes can be seen lined up outside the cabin doors. But we're due for some sunshine and hot air by the end of the week, and the children will no doubt spend a good part of the day in the lake.
  We ask each child's counselor to write a letter to the parents by the end of the second week of camp and again before your visit. It's a way for you to get a more personal explanation of how your child is doing and what activities s/he is involved in. Please call us if you have any concerns. At the end of the season, you will receive both an activity report and a cabin report, which will explain in more detail your child's strengths, weaknesses, and progress at camp.

And, rest assured, you will receive letters from us every now and then to fill you in on major camp events.

We suggest that parents write to their children at least twice a week—short, chatty letters that catch them up on major events at home. Although this is a time for the children to assert their independence, they can only be so brave if they receive support from their family. Even brief notes to say hello with a piece of gum in the envelope puts them at ease.

We recommend that you book your reservations at a local lodge at least two weeks in advance of the time you intend to visit. New Hampshire grows crowded in the summer even though there's no skiing.

Best wishes,

Harold and Lucy Reston

July 4

Dear Benjamin,

Happy Fourth of July! I'll bet the fireworks up there are spectacular, especially over the mountains on a dark night. Did the camp have a big celebration? Daddy found your sparklers in your drawer this morning. Sorry we forgot to pack them, but I'm sure one of the other children was able to share with you.

How was that long bus ride? We were hoping to get a postcard or something from you when you arrived. I hope no one got sick on the bus. Do you like the other children at camp? How many boys are in your bunk? Do you like them? What sorts of activities have you tried? Is the lake beautiful, and how well did you do on your swimming test?

Daddy has been very busy at the office and is working hard. We had dinner with the Kaufmans last night, which was fun. Hannah says she misses you and wants to talk to you the next time we call. She'll be spending this weekend at Grandma and Grandpa's house, so she won't be here for this first call (you'll hear from us before this letter arrives, I'm sure).

Daddy says he'll write soon.

I Love You!

Mommy

July 10

Dear Benjamin,

Wow, has it been hot in the city. We've been sweating in 100°
heat for almost a week now. The air conditioner in Daddy's office
broke and he had to close the office for two days. I imagine that it is
cool and beautiful in New Hampshire. How is the lake? You must
spend a lot of time swimming. Do they have you swim every day
when it's so hot?

Kirk was sick and we had to take him to the vet. Don't worry,
he's fine—just a small infection, and we have to give him pills twice
a day. They quiet him down, believe it or not, so he barks less when
cars make noise outside, and that makes Daddy happy since he can't
stand that yap yap yapping early in the morning.

We were very sad that we couldn't get through to you on the
phone on Sunday. I know you were expecting us to call, but the line
was busy before lunch and we went shopping in the afternoon.
We'll certainly speak this week, though. I hope that didn't
disappoint you too much. Hannah says she's writing you a letter.

Daddy says hello and will write.

I Love You!

Mommy

DEAR SCumBAG,

how IS CAMp? dO YOU
  like it? GRandmas wAS FUN and
theY BOUGHT me a dawn doll and
a hair-do JESSE.

I Made HER PUNK. she has
PINK hair and a STud on hER nose.
DADdy is takinG ME to the Beech

    anD I got SUN glasses
FOR IT. Kirk got

SICK IN MY Room. it was groSS.
we maDE
ORIGamy in
camp bUT Mine sucked. DINA made a
goOD one.

I toOK your meTZ hat to CAMP
on our field TRIP.

I HAVE A New name. its
        LEMON afTer THe beatles

GUY So dont

cAll me hannah BECAUSE I wont

look at you.

bye DOODY!
LEMON ANNE SHERMAN THE 1

July 13, 1994

Dear Mr. and Mrs. Sherman,

Chris and I are Benjamin's counselors this summer,
and we wanted to let you know how he's adjusting to
camp. He seems to be getting along well with the other
boys. Benjamin was very helpful on our overnight trip
gathering wood and blowing on the fire. So far he's been
interested in ceramics and shop, and he likes to watch
the other kids play softball. He has a little trouble
keeping his bed and cubbies neat, but I have helped teach
him to fold his clothes and stack them in piles.

Benjamin takes his toy letter with him to meals and
activities, and this has caused some of the other children
to comment. They ask him questions, and I think that
Benjamin may be a bit annoyed at this. We suggested that
Elliot remain at camp while we went out on our
overnight trip and Benjamin didn't argue, but Elliot came
with us to the lean-to anyway and got a little wet.

So far this looks like it will be a terrific summer for
Benjamin. He's already busy with projects and is a
unique member of the cabin group. We will write again
before mid-season, and we look forward to meeting you
when you visit.

Sincerely,

Dave McHugh

Camp Onianta
Bear Mountain Road
Fairfield, New Hampshire 03766
(603) 339-4109

Harold and Lucy Reston, Directors

July 14, 1994

Dear Mr. and Mrs. Sherman,

   The concerns you expressed about Benjamin in your questionnaire were very helpful to us, and we wanted to write you a note to inform you about Benjamin's experience so far at camp. Indeed, he is a quiet boy, but a very sensitive one no doubt, and he is an integral member of the cabin group. He takes direction without objection and attends all of his scheduled activities. We are concerned, however, about his attachment to his stuffed toy, and we hope that you can participate in our effort to separate him from Elliot.

   Benjamin takes Elliot with him all around camp, and it has caused some of the other children some discomfort. We were alerted to this potential problem by Dr. Dysan, and the matter grows increasingly disturbing. We understand both the cause of and need for this imaginary friend, and we are not qualified to speculate on the "normalcy" of this friendship, but it is clear to us that Elliot hinders Benjamin's growth and social development. For example, Benjamin talks to Elliot rather than his cabin mates, and this only serves to intensify his shy and introverted tendencies.

One of our goals for Benjamin this summer is that he become able to form relationships with children and that he feel more comfortable in social situations. But Elliot is an obstacle to the process.

We would very much like to speak with you about this matter when you visit. Perhaps you could suggest to Benjamin that Elliot return home with you for the rest of the summer. Please let us know your feelings on this. We do not intend to alter the course of your child's development— we strive to be a vehicle which he can use to grow.

Best wishes,

Harold Reston

July 20, 1994

Dear Benjamin,

Daddy and I received a wonderful letter from your counselors today. They said that you were doing well at camp and had made lots of friends with other boys. It sounds as though you are busy working on your projects. Daddy asked how you were doing on your swimming card—have you gotten to Intermediate yet? Did you get a letter from Hannah? I know she'd love to hear from you, so please write to her. Daddy and I would like to hear from you too. It's so hard to talk on the phone with all the other kids around. What are you enjoying at camp? What are your friends' names? Daddy and I are excited to meet them. Perhaps you would like to invite one or two of them on a picnic with us. We will bring you some surprises.

Daddy and I feel very strongly that Elliot does not leave the cabin. We can talk about this on the phone. You had agreed to leave Elliot at home for the summer, and we thought that was a wonderful idea. You and I have talked about this, and I know that Dr. Dysan has discussed it with you as well. Please stick to our agreement, at least until our next phone call, and we will talk about this then.

Did you find your blue sweatshirt? It's probably in the back of your cubby—please look for it. I sewed your name on the hood, so it should be returned to you in the lost and found. We will see you in little over a week.

Hugs and kisses!
XXX OOO

Mommy

Mid-late July . . . Does anybody really know what time it is?

To: Ron, the king of summer sun absorbency.

From: Dave, the anemic-looking, underpaid asshole who baby-sits eighteen hours a day.

Yo Ron,

What's up? How's life at the Cape? Are you loving it? Is it the wild social scene you expected? I'm giving you one more week at that job and then you'll quit—I'm putting money on it. I don't get to do a whole lot of beach hopping up here. They keep us pretty busy. Get the kids up at 7:30 — shit, can't believe I'm getting up at 7:30 — cabin cleanup by 9:00, then four periods teaching sports. I get a free period every day, and rest hour is definitely the best time of all. Power nap. Days off are pretty awesome. We drive to the Radisson Hotel in West Lebanon and drink beer by the pool late at night. There's a bar about four miles down the road from camp and sometimes we go pound during a free period.

I really lucked out with my co-counselor. His name is Chris Ryder and he's from Wisconsin, and he's really cool. We get along really well, except that I do most of the busy work while he keeps up with the horses.

And the kids are pretty cute. Yes—I actually do think that kids are cute and not just obnoxious! We've got nine of them in the cabin—they're about twelve or so and their hormones are going crazy and that kind of shit. I got to give them this big sex/jerking off lecture the other night, and they were too wired to sleep. They were laughing and rolling around and whispering to each other. This one kid knew everything already, though, and that blew my mind. He's only twelve, and he knows more about sex than I do! Actually he's a pretty weird animal all around. The kids call him Spacefuck. His name is Benjamin, and he carries around a stuffed letter wherever he goes. He's kind of a freaky kid. He never talks to anyone and pets the dirt on the road. Actually, he said more about jerking off than he has about anything else since he got here. The directors are getting a little aggravated at him—and he makes me nuts a lot of the time. Sometimes I just can't deal.

Then there's the kid who shits in his pants—that's a real treat. Him I got to deal with. And now Benjamin started shitting in his pants too. You should smell this cabin. It's unbelievable. Then there's this kid named Mark, and all he says is mutherfucker. Yes, mutherfucker, or that mutherfucker, or how you doing, mutherfucker. They're not supposed to curse really, but I set a pretty crappy example. And we have three Peters, so I gave them numbers. Peter 1 is great. He'll be a stud in a year or so—slick hair, hi-tops, you know what I mean. Maybe we'll hang out when he's legal.

So I guess you could say I've made the rounds here.
I got pretty tight with the ceramics counselor. She's
not that great-looking but she's nice and has really
muscular legs. But that didn't really turn into
anything. I don't know—the people here are pretty
tame. Most of them couple up and stay that way.
There's not a whole lot of scamming going on, so I
guess I was pretty lucky to get anything. Now there's
only four people going out, and everyone else is
looking at everyone else. I'm kind of not in the mood,
though. I like the guys a lot, and we pound Coors and
watch movies. It's pretty cool.

You should road trip up here some weekend and we
can party. It's a cool scene, and there's a girl who is
a Type A prospect. Her name's Diana, and I told her
about you. She's not into me, and I think Chris might
be into her but he won't admit it, so get your ass in
the car and jam.

Take care—you studly tan animal!

Dave

July 22

Dear Benjamin,

Only a few days until we see your cute face. Daddy and I miss you very much and can't wait to visit. We can't wait to hear what you've been doing at camp so far. Why don't you invite one of your friends on a picnic with us? Tell him to bring a bathing suit and we'll all go in the lake.

I can't find Elliot's coat, Benjamin. I know you told me it was in the front closet, but I don't see it there. I'm sure that Elliot doesn't need a cover in this heat anyway. And we will have to talk about Elliot when we get to camp. I thought I made it clear to you on the phone that Elliot must stay on your bed. We will discuss this when I see you.

XXX OOO

Mom

July 22, 1994

Dear Mr. and Mrs. Sherman,

We understand that you will be visiting camp on the
30th, and we are eager to have a chance to speak with
you.

Benjamin is still busy with his ceramics project and he
goes to all the softball games, but he has completely
stopped talking to his peers. He talks to Elliot still, but
he won't respond to anyone else. This has been a little
frustrating for us. He listens and he is responsible in the
cabin, but we have a hard time trying to include him in
cabin activities.

Yesterday, Benjamin pushed one of his bunkmates off a
bicycle. The incident occurred without any warning, and
was upsetting to the other boy. Twice this week,
Benjamin has been unable to make it to the bathroom,
which embarrassed him. The nurse examined him and
gave him some medicine, but she does not think that he
is sick or anything. Chris and I are afraid that he is
unhappy here, and we have discussed this with the
Restons.

One evening last week, Benjamin lost Elliot. We found
him rocking on his bed as the children were getting
ready to go to sleep, and we discovered that Elliot was
not with him. We found Elliot a few hours later, buried
beneath clothes and papers under his bed. But the
incident was very upsetting for Benjamin. At least it
didn't turn out to be anything serious.

We'd like to arrange for Benjamin to spend time in the

ceramics room during your visit so that the four of us will have a chance to talk privately. Have a good trip to New Hampshire, and we look forward to meeting you.

Sincerely,

Dave McHugh
Chris Ryder

Camp Onianta
Bear Mountain Road
Fairfield, New Hampshire 03766
(603) 339-4109

Harold and Lucy Reston, Directors

July 23, 1994

Dear Mr. and Mrs. Sherman,
  *We were very glad that you telephoned us last week—
we feel it's important for us to know what you think your
child is feeling. And we are very sorry that Benjamin has
not written to you yet. We ask counselors to collect letters
home twice a week, and we will ask Benjamin's
counselors to encourage Benjamin to write.*

  *The issues we mentioned in our last letter to you have
both intensified and become more noticeable. Whereas
Benjamin's stuffed toy did not seem to be problematic,
it has become an issue of some concern. Benjamin
uses the toy as a vehicle through which he can avoid
communicating and participating with his peers. It
has become an obstacle more than a simple comfort.*

  *We have asked Dave and Chris, Benjamin's counselors,
to send you a letter describing Benjamin's behavior in
somewhat more detail. They have been able to form a
closer relationship to him than we have, and they are
able to see things that camp directors sometimes miss.*

We hope to arrange a brief meeting between the six of us when you visit.

All the best,

Harold and Lucy Reston

August 1

Dear Benjamin,

We had a wonderful day with you at camp and thought the camp was beautiful. Your counselors seem very friendly and they like you a great deal. I wish that you had shown me your ceramics project, but I'm sure you'll show it to me when you get home. What a beautiful lake they have at Onianta! The weather was perfect for our visit. I would have loved to get some pictures of you in the water.

On our way home from camp we stopped at Grandma and Grandpa's house for a day. Hannah was very tired and slept most of the way in the car. It rained the whole way back and we had to eat at a fast-food restaurant on the highway. I hope you enjoy the treats Daddy and I brought you. The cookies must be stale by now, but the nuts are in a tin so they'll stay fresh. You might want to share some of your gifts with your close friends.

Elliot is resting on your bed along the wall and seems very comfortable. It's better for Elliot to be home—that way no bugs and dirt will get stuck in the material, and Elliot won't get handled by other children or lost in the woods. It's much better this way for everybody. I'm sure the Restons will talk about this decision with you.

I hope you'll find time to write to me during this half of the summer. Daddy and I would love to get a letter from you. We will call you next Sunday, and I hope I get a letter from you by then.

Hugs and kisses, kisses and hugs,

XO

Mom

August 1, 1994

Harold and Lucy Reston
Camp Onianta
Bear Mountain Road
Fairfield, New Hampshire 03766

Dear Harold and Lucy,

Jeffrey and I were grateful to have the opportunity to speak with you at length. Of course, Benjamin's social adjustment is of great concern to us, and we feel relieved knowing that he has personal attention and such care. As Jeffrey told you, we are not surprised that Benjamin is having trouble, and Jeffrey thought it would be a good idea to withdraw him from Onianta. But our discussion changed our minds, and we think that Benjamin might make some improvements this summer. Certainly this month without Elliot will test his strength. It was both heartbreaking and relieving to take Elliot away from Benjamin, and now we know it is an important move. Maybe Benjamin will want to be with his bunkmates now and participate in group activities instead of private projects.

In any event, thank you for your patience, concern, and attention. I feel very safe entrusting Benjamin to you—both his physical and social well-being are obviously in good hands. We will call you after we speak to Benjamin next week. Please let us know if any changes take place.

Warmly,

Peggy Sherman

August 1

To: Ron, the ray-o-sun who gets paid to serve cute
girls gin and tonics.
From: The guy with nine children and no woman and
no money.

Hey—

I was psyched to get your call. You caught me in
the middle of a staff meeting, which was a prime
move—They're really boring as shit and they go on
forever. We talk about problem kids and how to
handle them and stuff like that, and it just goes on
and on. So it's key to get phone calls during staff
meetings because it gets you out of the scene for a
while. You sounded awesome. I'm jealous of your all-
play-no-work lifestyle. Sorry you guys broke up. She
was pretty cool. But she did get uptight about a lot of
shit. And at least now you don't have to feel guilty.

Bartending, huh? Not bad. They must not have
asked your age, so they must be either desperate or
lame. I can't believe you get to sleep in until 1:00. By
1:00 here I have woken up, washed and dressed all my
kids, had an energetic breakfast conversation with
other kids—you know how much I love to talk at
breakfast—forced a half dozen aspirin down my
throat to kill a wicked hangover, cleaned up a rancid
cabin and folded three thousand dirty tee-shirts,
umped a softball game, taught little girls tennis,

40

taken hyper kids to the lake for a swim, biked a few miles to get the camp mail, played with gray meat loaf or purple pork chops on my lunch plate, and hollered at my kids for twenty minutes so they'll shut up for rest hour. The thing that saves me when I just think I'm going to keel over is this one girl I think I mentioned on the phone. She's the drama counselor and she's really funny in staff meetings and she smiles at me a lot. I can get into that.

Actually, I think I make camp sound much worse than it really is. It's actually a lot of fun, but I'm glad it's only for two months.

I'm tired as hell here, though. It makes 8:30 a.m. classes look like no big shit. There's just no time to sleep, and the kids are really demanding. I like working with them a lot, though. I had this play wrestling match with one of the older kids a few days ago, and it was wild. He tried so hard to pin me, so I let him. It must have made his month. I'm sick as shit of cookouts, though. They really suck. The deal is the kids sit around the fire and giggle and the counselors make the fire and cook burgers and hand out chocolate milk. I smell like ashes for the rest of the night. We made pizza bagels in the kitchen one time, which was a relief. One kid — the one who never says anything and fondles a stuffed letter H — really got off on those pizza bagels. So did the one who shits in his pants. And Peter 1 offered to wash the dishes. He's my man. We play softball 700 during free periods and he catches all my pop flies. Then all the other kids want to play too, except the letter-fondling freak, who likes to sit and watch and giggle his little fool head off. His parents were up last week, and they were really strange. You've seen it before — the nervous mother and the father on another planet. And his sister changed her name to Cantaloupe or Kiwi or Artichoke or some other goddamn fruit or vegetable freak thing. I swear, this kid is doomed to be the class misfit for life — it's amazing how you can tell that kind of shit. He did a really awesome imitation of me and the things I say, and phrases I use like rocking and rad and lame and you know all the words I use a lot. I laughed for a while and thought about doing an imitation of him, but it would have hurt his feelings and I didn't want to cope with a paranoid misfit with a bruised ego. Most of the parents have been friendly, and some of them even give me food. They're not allowed to give me money, but Christ knows I deserve it.

So you've got to come up and meet the staff. They're a really cool group, and my co-counselor is a blast. We don't go to that bar as much, but after midnight we drink a few beers in the main house. The kids will love you because you're blond and you can swing the bat with one arm. Call again on either a Sunday or Wednesday night after 9:00 so I can bag on another staff meeting.

Dave

August 9, 1994

Dear Benjamin,

Please write to Mommy and Daddy and tell us what you're doing at camp. You must be busy-busy now that the halfway mark is over. Are you almost done with your ceramics project? What will you do next? How are your bunkmates, and that one named Peter who Daddy liked so much? Are the two of you good friends?

Hannah was a little upset that you wouldn't call her Lemon when we came to visit. She wrote the name Lemon on her door, and Daddy and I punished her for writing on the walls. Now her room is lemon everything—stickers and erasers and posters and bubble gum! I don't know why she chose this name, and Grandma and Grandpa don't understand. They would like to get a letter from you since they haven't seen you in a while. Elliot is still sitting on your bed next to the stuffed A and the S. I'm sure they're all very happy to have each other's company.

I wish you could find the sweatshirt, Benjamin. I'll mail you a new one since it gets cold at night there, but please look around for it. We will call you on Sunday.

XO XO

Mommy

August 14

Dear Benjamin,

So the summer is almost over, sweetheart, and I hope it has been rewarding for you in many ways. Take advantage of these last few weeks to do different things—new things—things you haven't tried to do yet. Try to do things you never thought you could do, and you'll feel good about yourself for doing them. And Daddy and I will be so proud of you.

Your sister is almost done with day camp, too, and she has lots of pretty projects to show you. And she has made some new friends who I'm sure you will like. She can't wait to go shopping for school supplies and a new bookbag, but I thought I'd wait for you to come home and we can all do it together. Are you looking forward to school? It will seem strange at first to sleep in your own room— you're so used to sleeping with lots of friends all around, and I'll bet being home will seem so quiet to you. But you'll be able to have sleepovers with camp friends when you want to.

Daddy is in California on a business trip and he'll be back on Thursday. So it's just been me and Hannah puttering around the house. We are excited to see you, and will have pizza for dinner on the first night.

I Love You,

Mom

Date: August 14. I know this because I've been a new
man since August 4.

Time: Time for me to get my shit together. Time is an
illusion. Time has too much light and not
enough night.

Ron—

Things are really good. I've gotten into this girl.
Her name is Diana and she's older. She's a senior and
she teaches drama here. She's cool. I think you'd like
her. She's funny and pretty laid back and really cute
when she's drunk. She gets really turned on when
she's plastered and we almost did it on a picnic table
outside the bar. She's really into me, which is weird
because I never thought she'd consider going out with
me, but some people told me she was looking at me a
lot at a staff party. So we went out walking and my
flashlight broke and she said that was just about as
lame a trick as if my car ran out of gas on the
highway. But I wasn't scamming so I laughed and then
I kissed her and she liked it. So this is a good thing. I
don't know about after the summer. She's more
serious than I am, and I can't see myself driving to
Wesleyan every weekend to see a girl. We have a
good time together. Sometimes when we have a free
period together we go back to this bar and have a
beer, or we sit outside on the green and sleep for a
few minutes. And on our night off we went to this

bed-and-breakfast in Woodstock. Everything was really good. It was a cool time.

Yesterday was hike day and we were on different hikes and it was crazy—I couldn't stop thinking about her. I just kept replaying those tapes in my head, you know what I mean? I remember everything, and you know I never remember anything. And the kids were all tired and cranky and it just didn't bother me. I carried all the food for the hike and the kids' wet towels (we went brook-slopping), and the kid with the letter had a huge knapsack filled with rocks and paper which he could barely get on his shoulder so I carried all his shit, and then this girl cut her foot so I carried her for a little while, and it just didn't matter. I couldn't wait to get back to camp. I had Chris put the kids to bed so Diana and I could hang out. I didn't get back to the cabin until it was light out.

So what do you think? I told a friend from high school, and he said he can't picture me with a girlfriend. Neither can I. But now I guess I've got one. It sort of freaks me out. She's the same age as my sister. Maybe you'll get to meet her. I'll call you when I get back to New York.

Dave

DEAR BENJamIN SHERman

MY NAME is still LEMON like I TOLD you
in mY OTHer
letteR AND when I CAME to your Camp. I
will not
    let YOU INTo my room IF YOU
CALL me by THAT OTHer name.

Your CAMP Looked FUN BUt you dont have
ORAGAmy
AND I am good at that.
        YOU were WEIRD when we
came and VISITed and
sometimes it was BORING.
        PIZZA bagles SOUNDS GOOD.
mommy
put your TOY LETTERs on

thE FLoor WHEN SHE Was cleening

up anD I TOLD Her you wouldnt like that

and THEY ARE on the bed

now. DID YOU know thEY were
          COMing to take one home. I said it
was   mean BecAUSE IF They ever took my
BROWNY
bear or my HAIR-do jesse id
thrOW A fit at them.
          I THINK YOU SHOULD have THrown
a FIT AT Them likE I WOULd but oh
well its TO LATE NOW. no GOOD TO CRY
over   spild miLK LIKE daddy said. I
GESS I'LL SEE YOU

PRetty soon
love sweet john LEMON

Camp Onianta
Bear Mountain Road
Fairfield, New Hampshire 03766
(603) 339-4109

Harold and Lucy Reston, Directors

August 24, 1994

Dear Parents,

It's hard to believe that the summer is over, and what a season it has been: a summer filled with challenges to meet and successful achievements. Almost every child swam the lake this summer—the most since the camp first began. There were new projects built in the shop—a table with drawers out of wood, a leather shoulder bag with a matching wallet, checkbook cover, and belt, a thick and finely filed bell made out of silver.

The musical was a delight and the cast included over thirty children. We had counselors share their life stories during campfires each week and perform skits with children during Amateur Night—a staff and camper talent show. There was a lot of rain in August. The staff did some quick thinking and came up with new indoor activities, but mud slides were the usual favorite. Only one hike was rained out, and some of the trips the kids completed were incredible—one mountain hike left before the rising bell and didn't return until long after supper. Overnighters were a mixed bag. They left just as the stomach bug was settling in, and a few campers spent the second night in the infirmary. But they were all well enough to participate in the softball league playoffs, and the finals lasted ten innings!

We have enclosed your child's activity reports—a short statement by the counselors of each activity about your child's participation and particular interests. Also enclosed is a cabin report—a longer letter written by your child's cabin counselors about his or her involvement in the cabin, favorite activities, special achievements, and problems to conquer. The cabin report may include recommendations for next summer. If you have any questions or would like to discuss any issues that are raised, please do not hesitate to call us. We will be in New Hampshire wrapping mattresses and storing flatware until the second week of September.

Again, much pride should be felt about the past eight weeks, and we hope to see all of you at the reunion in January.

All the best,

Harold and Lucy Reston

Onianta

August 24, 1994

ACTIVITY REPORTS

Benjamin Sherman

Archery Benjamin attended archery with his cabin when scheduled and earned a Junior Yeoman pin early in the summer.

Drama Benjamin participated in improvisation games a great deal. He played drama games with his cabin and during his free periods as well. Benjamin seemed to enjoy scenes which involved two people and a given conflict, and when he couldn't resolve the situation he said "Beam me up Scotty" and the exercise was over. But Benjamin seemed to love theater games and was able to laugh affectionately at himself and his peers. He did an incredible imitation of his counselor during one improvisation exercise, and the details he recalled and performed make me quite certain that Benjamin has great potential in drama.

Ceramics Benjamin spent a great deal of time in the ceramics shop, although he showed little interest in learning new skills or developing an ability with the wheel. He worked long and hard on a project which involved different shades of clay, varnish, and etching tools. He would not tell me what it was he invented, but he worked furiously at it and seemed extremely pleased with its completion.

Shop   Shop was a favorite activity for Benjamin. He worked on projects in woodworking and leather.

Swim   Benjamin was reluctant to participate in swim when scheduled.

Riflery   Benjamin loved riflery this summer and won many awards during the season.

Sports   Benjamin chose not to focus on athletics at Onianta, but he was an encouraging spectator for the softball league.

Boating   Benjamin loved the single-man kayaks and spent a lot of time paddling himself around a small island in the middle of the lake.

Music   Although Benjamin did not learn to play an instrument, he did sing camp songs in the evening.

Art   Benjamin worked hard on one art project—a detailed and color-coded map for which he needed to use a compass, colored pencils, and stencils. But at the end of the summer, he poured water on the map and it looked destroyed. Nevertheless, he let the paper dry and seemed satisfied with his project.

Nature   Benjamin had a quiet interest in nature. He was one of the few campers who chose to attend Nature, and he'd ask a lot of complex questions about the formation of rocks and streams and the natural process of decay. And Benjamin noticed a great deal about the natural world—he'd often stop to gather rocks or small animals or odd-shaped leaves. It was a pleasure to watch Benjamin discover nature and the outdoors, and I hope his interest continues as he grows older.

Electronics Benjamin built a walkie-talkie set out of a kit in electronics.

Riding Benjamin participated in riding when scheduled with his cabin but showed no exceptional interest in the sport.

Sewing Toward the end of the summer, Benjamin developed a sudden interest in sewing. He put together a stuffed toy in the shape of an H out of old pieces of felt, stuffed it with cotton, and sewed the edges together by hand. He expressed interest in sewing more stuffed letters. Hopefully he'll be able to do this next year.

August 24, 1994

Dear Mr. and Mrs. Sherman,
 This has certainly been a memorable summer for
Benjamin, as he was an integral, unique member of the
cabin group as well as the Onianta community. In the
cabin, Benjamin had respect for his bunkmates. He never
interfered with their belongings, as he kept his own
separate. He had a tendency to "put things away" under
his bed. He loved to build fires for cabin cookouts. He
was a great deal of help when the group cooked pizza
bagels in the kitchen—in fact, Benjamin made pizza
bagels for everybody. He also sang to us during mountain
climbing hikes and entertained the group with Eddie
Murphy jokes and skits.
 Sometimes Benjamin had trouble sleeping, particularly
at the very beginning of the summer and immediately
following your visit. This is only natural during a major
separation, but it caused Benjamin some additional
discomfort during the day. He preferred to sleep by
himself near the brook rather than participating in group
activities. He also insisted upon quiet during rest hour
and became a vicious letter writer.
 We think that Benjamin made some significant strides
this summer. He became friendly with his bunkmates. He
was more able to become involved in group activities and
seemed to spend less time by himself. And toward the
end he was often seen with a girl during sings and
campfires and free time between periods. He let us know
when he needed to use the bathroom and was able to

structure his free time extremely well. Benjamin
concentrated in ceramics and constructed a major project
I'm sure he'll bring home to show you.

With regards to next summer, it is difficult to know
what to say. It looks as though Benjamin had a good time
at Onianta, but since he rarely speaks it is difficult to
actually confirm this. And even though he became more
comfortable in social circumstances, he still exhibited odd
behaviors in front of his peers. These included talking to
himself, even when Elliot was brought home, writing
furiously, rocking back and forth, playing intensely with
the dirt, laughing when he was alone, sitting in the
middle of the athletic field while other children played
softball, or refusing to move his arms during swimming.
Benjamin ate very little and was reluctant to change his
clothes. He certainly wasn't antagonistic to his cabin
mates or intentionally breaking group concentration, but
other children had trouble understanding his behavior.
We cannot tell if Benjamin ever felt successful or even at
ease here. Even though his actions changed as the
summer went on, particularly after your visit, he was
consistently withdrawn.

Perhaps a summer away from Onianta will prove
whether or not he would choose to be here.

Yours truly,

Dave McHugh
Chris Ryder

Camp Onianta
Bear Mountain Road
Fairfield, New Hampshire 03766
(603) 339-4109

Harold and Lucy Reston, Directors

August 31, 1994

Dear Mr. and Mrs. Sherman,

Benjamin's counselors found a blue sweatshirt, a hiking boot, and a stack of papers underneath his bed. We have enclosed his belongings along with a list of items Benjamin purchased at the camp store. Please send a check for the amount specified on the attached page.

All the best,

Harold and Lucy Reston

Benjamin Sherman

6/30	Stamps	$5.80
	Flashlight	$5.75
	Batteries	$2.50
7/5	Mess Kit	$4.00
	Canteen	$2.00
	Insect repellent	$1.75
7/17	Batteries	$2.50
7/29	Stamps	$5.80
	Paper	$0.95
	Envelopes	$0.95
8/5	Paper	$0.95
	Envelopes	$0.95
8/10	Paper	$1.90
	Envelopes	$1.90
8/16	Batteries	$2.50
8/18	Paper	$1.90
	Envelopes	$1.90

_____

TOTAL $44.00

PART
TWO

Letters
Under
the Bed

On the evening of the day eta 2, on the last day of the old life and first day of your new life, dear Elliot, There is not much for me to say to you except that I am crying and I know you will be good and fine at my home. Please write to me because I am receiving very soft transmissions from the planet Elliottown. I will write again soon.

Star date supplemental dear Elliot, When the parent creatures came to visit it was bad. I wish they let you come around camp with us because I would have felt much better and maybe even done some of the things they wanted me to do. You should not take what they say about you personally. It is true that they do not like you, but that is not your fault. Alot of people do not like me and that's not supposed to be my fault either, so you shouldn't feel bad like I don't feel bad. They just don't understand Elliots, and people don't like the things they don't understand. That's how prejudice starts and they are now prejudiced against you but you and I know better than that. All the parental units wanted to do was watch me swim and play softball. They brought lunch even though I told them on the phone that I would make pizza bagels. They didn't give anything to Dave and Chris and a lot of other mothers did. They should have given something to Dave because he is very nice and never makes me do stuff and he loves Eddie Murphy. They should have brought him cheese and stuff so he could make more pizza bagels. Then he could have let me make them again and he loves pizza bagels like me. They brought me cookies in a tin but they took you away even though they asked me if they could and I said no. They did it anyway. I should have known they would. Why didn't you remind me that they would do that? I would have protected you. Elliots need bodyguards and children don't need parents. But I know you will never get mad at me. Dr. Dysan will be mad at us when we have to go back to him but we don't have to talk. You don't have to say anything if you don't want to Elliot and no human can listen in on your thoughts. But that is not soon. And it is not soon enough when it will be time to be, Benjamin.

On the day of theta 2 as the light leaves this planet to go to yours I am remaining dear Elliot, This is not as bad as it was when I thought I lost you because now at least I know where you are. When you disappeared I bowed very hard to INVISIBLE ELLIOT to have you found. I thought maybe you had been taken to a bad planet or something. So I bowed and bowed and spoke the language of Elliottown and just thought about you Elliot and all the Elliots very very hard. And it worked. You appeared under my bed and I knew that I had done good work. They were testing me I bet. And I passed and I won and you and I can be together, but now we are apart and if this is a new test it is very hard. Much has happened since you departed even though your exit was recent. It has grown cold here. The light leaves much earlier and I must use an electronic light stick to write, but I am not allowed to illuminate it after the other earthlings are in bed, so I must write these in front of them outside. I have done some good things. I have read The Enemy Within and enjoyed it. I have almost finished the buried treasure pieces. I have learned to build fires in case we need warmth, and I can solder metal so it can transmit energy. I have met a person that we might be able to trust with information about Elliottown. Her name is Amelia and she is one hundred and nineteen months old. Nobody talks to her either. She likes movie stars and drama and playing with her hair and she likes to wear shorts in the rain and skirts on hike days. She likes to dance but sits down sometimes and talks alot. I like her and people think that we are boyfriend and girlfriend and we are sort of that but not really. I don't care how far you get with girls and a peck on the cheek is fine. She asked me where you were and I said you were taken back to my room and she was sad. Do you think I should tell her some stuff? Maybe just a little to test her and see how she reacts.

Until it is time to be, Benjamin.

On the day of iota 2 dear Benjamin, This is what I know. My armlegs were suddenly grasped by a human hand which secured me first beneath an armpit and then in a crowded vinyl bag with citrus-smelling life-sustaining remnants. My new casing was bumped and left alone for a while until it was thrown into the colder, locked portion of a moving vehicle. The part that humans gain access to from the rear only. Then the moving vehicle moved slowly, then the moving vehicle moved faster, making weight shifts and directional changes without warning. This went on for 360 minutes and then I was taken out of the colder locked compartment of the moving vehicle and brought inside what your female parent tells you to call home. Antares and Sherman greeted me with some surprise but also they were happy. Of course the greeting was silent. The female put my physical structure next to them, but my mental component was planning to go to Elliottown. Antares, Sherman and I are not worried about you. We do not worry like the others but we do think hard about you.

Until it is time to be, Elliot.

On the day after iota 2, also known as kappa 2 dear Elliot, I have received your letter. I am sorry the transport to where my female parent tells me to call home was so unpleasant. It is good that you are making mental plans to go to Elliottown. I will find a way to find out what is going on there. We need a new Elliot. I will have to construct an Elliot for me here. But now I have to go. At one hour post mid day nutrition supplement I have dramatics, and then I must do some work on the ceramics project.

Until it is time to be, Benjamin.

In answer to your words on theta 2, on the day of lambda 2 as the light leaves at the same time in my place as it does in yours dear Benjamin, First I will address your other letter to me. You must use the light stick. You have to keep writing. If the others do not allow it, go outside and illuminate the light stick in a safe hiding place. No human should interfere with the necessary operations of Elliots and Elliottown. The Enemy Within is indeed a good book. My favorite is still Tholian's Web. When you come home we can watch the visual version together. There are some problems with Amelia. She is very bouncy. She is like Tigger the tiger from Winnie the Pooh. And she talks to people all the time even when they tell her that they want her to be quiet. You have learned Benjamin that when people don't want to hear what you want to say then stop talking to them. You can always talk to me because I never don't want to hear what you want to say. Amelia has not learned this. I am a little afraid that she will talk about Elliots. There are some things that humans should not know. It does not matter to me that nobody likes Amelia. They must not know her, because she is easy to like. And if they do not like her then they are subnormal and stupid and not worth being near. It might be nice to do more than a peck on the cheek or lips. Do you remember what Kirk does to the green figure? You might want to try that. But not too much because if you are bad at it she'll know you haven't practiced. But she might not have practiced either. You should get to know her more and better.

Until it is time to be, Elliot.

On the day of mu 2, commonly known as the 3 day of August
Dear Elliot, I am sure that you are doing alright at home. I am
sorry I cannot be with you, but I am thinking of you, and I know
that Antares and Sherman are happy to be with you. Soon you
will be able to go back to Elliottown and help all the Elliots
through the dark season. Then you can be at home in the fourth
dimension and travel through spacetime for a while. I have been
told that since you left, the economic peak has lessened and
some of the Elliots are hurting badly. They have been bowing very
hard to INVISIBLE ELLIOT and since he is good he will keep them
from starving. Since I have made that new friend called Amelia I
have also made a new friend for you. Her name is Evelyn and
she is your configuration but in different colors. I made her out of
your coat which I told mother I lost but which I kept under the bed
with your letters, and I have made the coat into a duplicate of
you. I suspect that mother would try to get all the Elliots out of my
life so I hid your coat and told her it was in Connecticut but it was
really here with me. So that way I could make another Elliot and
she would never know that I could or that I did that. Evelyn will be
a good Elliot and they will like her in Elliottown. And it is good
that she is another female. I thought you might mind being the
only female for so long and now the two of you can split up the
things females need to do. Antares and Sherman, you will like
Evelyn too. I'll bet you're glad to be with Elliot again. Make sure
she is not too sad without me to talk to her. Please keep writing to
me so that I know what is happening. Do you have any ideas
about where I should set the buried treasure pieces? I am glazing
them now and soon the counselor figure will put them in the kiln
again. Write to me and tell me where you think I should put the
coded rocks. You know the camp grounds well and are familiar
with the stream.
Until it is time to be, Benjamin.

Four days past iota 2 also known as the day of nu in the year 500,000 in Elliottown commonly known now as the 4th day of August in the Christian year 1994 dear Benjamin, While you were gathering information about Elliottown I have been there and returned. You are exactly right about things there as you always are. The dark season comes quickly. Some of the small Elliots are lonely and one of them got a soft blue tribble but was told to dispose of it since it multiplies so quickly. Elliottown would become tribbletown in no time. And the economic peak is fast turning into an economic disaster. Nobody is making food and the markets are empty and people do not leave their homes anymore. Yes INVISIBLE ELLIOT is good and strong but very slow to respond now. I think that he is very depressed that you and I are not together, and when INVISIBLE ELLIOT is depressed, all the Elliots are depressed too. And when people are depressed they like to stay home. Like the time Dr. Dysan the alien asked you if you were sad because you liked to stay home so much. I will go back to Elliottown today and try to do something. You decided to trust Amelia. I think that will be ok. She is very pretty. She is still bouncy. She loves peanut butter which is good. There is lots of peanut butter on Elliottown. Evelyn is a beautiful name. I could use another friend and it is nice to have a female one. And it is also good that she is the same H shape as I am. Antares and Sherman are fun and friendly, but the A and S shapes all in one space make it easy for us to get tangled up in each other and then it looks like we're doing something bad like Spock did to that woman on that planet with the spraying flowers or what you saw Dave doing with the drama lady. I still can't decide where to hide the buried treasure map. I'll keep processing it.
Until it is time to be, Elliot.

On the same day as your expected letter to me at a time of day with strong ultraviolet rays dear Benjamin, I just figured out where you can put the buried treasure map pieces. There are eight disks with different parts of the map, so here are eight hiding spots I once found in Onianta. Underneath the post which holds the fence and the dirt there is a small space. There are two rocks in the upper part of the brook with a funnel shape between them which will hold a disk perfectly. There is a lot of space beneath the office porch. Dig a hole there, the dirt is very wet and soft, and put a disk in the hole. Put a disk in a pile of blank rocks by the swimming dock. Put two in the bike shed. Put one by the campfire sight, and put the last one by slippery rock in the mama brook.

Please keep writing until it is time to be, Elliot.

On the day of omicron 2 as the radioactive waves make their first showing on the horizon Dear Elliot, I have heard there are some more problems in Elliottown. Evelyn is definitely a good Elliot and has visited the planet and is disturbed. Some of the Elliots are dying, and no Elliot can understand why. It may be that germs have spread in the world with no diseases, but how could they have come there. I am wondering if Mother's touch has interfered and sent germs on waves at the speed of light to Elliottown. We must find an antidote before all the Elliots die. I have not been able to contact Elliottown very much since Evelyn is very young and gets tired of traveling. I wonder if Mother's germs on the waves at the speed of light have contaminated INVISIBLE ELLIOT so that he can no longer function. What are your thoughts on this stuff? You are all safe at home, and you will be safer with me there.

Until it is time to be, Benjamin.

On the day of pi 2 after the letter of omicron 2 in emergency red alert Dear Benjamin, All of us Elliots are very concerned. Antares, Sherman and I have been to Elliottown. You are right. The Elliots are dying. We do not know why they are dying all of a sudden. Do you think that INVISIBLE ELLIOT is dying too? He might have been poisoned or something. We are very much alone on Earth. There can be no more Elliots here or too many people will know, and without an Elliottown, we will have no one to visit and no one to talk to and no playmates. I thought for a while that maybe the Thworks were up to some bad tricks. Maybe they are finally sick and tired of the strangeness of Elliots and have decided to kill us. I don't know why they think they are so great but they do, and they are bad to other species because they think so. It is because we like to wander instead of playing sports, and we like to read Star Trek books and go to conventions and they like to go far with girls. And we rub ourselves and they say it's disgusting but you know they do it too. And they like to put stuff in their hair and listen to Aerosmith and The Red Hot Chili Peppers and we like to keep our same set of clothes on and we don't like music. They dance with girls but we dance by ourselves. I think they have had enough of us. I will go back to Elliottown and try to help but I will not let the Elliots change to be like them.
Until it is time to be, Elliot.

On the day after your letter which means today is the day of rho 2 dear Elliot, I have done something bad. I don't know why I did a bad thing but I did it and I couldn't help it and now I feel bad. Maybe I did it because I was so upset about the dying Elliots on Elliottown. Remember that guy I pushed off the bike when you were here? It was when you and I were having an important meeting and he butts in and said mean things because he listened to us. He hates me now and I hate him back. This morning I was wandering around the softball field trying to think of what to do about missing you and saving the dying Elliots and he told me to stop walking in circles like a freak and get my ass off the softball field because he wanted to practice hitting. I didn't stop because I was there first and I was very busy. He yelled at me again and then some kids in my cabin helped him yell. So I walked off and stood by the backstop kicking the dirt to get me to think better. So he held the bat and said poor Benjamin without his spaceman has nothing to do and he swung the bat at me to fake me out so I jumped on top of him and sat on him and punched him a little. He called me a freak and a faggot and I bounced on him. And then Mark called me a mother fucker and I hate that so I took him on too. Dave saw me and pulled me off of him and yelled at all of us but mostly at me. I never saw Dave get mad at me or anybody else because he just gets tired but he was really mad at me. And then we had to see the nurse and the directors they were mad. Now it is fourth period and I am writing this to you when I should be playing tennis. H–shaped Elliots don't like playing tennis because they get confused about which arms to use. Now they all look at me funny.
I can't wait until it is time to be, Benjamin.

On the day after the letter of rho 2, composition date sigma 2 after a second emergency voyage to Elliottown dear Benjamin, Don't worry about what you did because there are more important things to worry about. What you did is bad like they said and you know that but you have to think about that another time and think now about some emergencies. Things are very very bad on our planet. Everything is out of order and a mess. I went back there with Antares and Sherman and they were shocked. There are Elliots running around everywhere. They look unfed and unhappy. INVISIBLE ELLIOT is no where to be found. I think he may have run off somewhere and the Elliots are going crazy. And I think it is because you and I are apart. They are not doing the things we used to do together like investigate the ground and laugh and make plans for the economy and they are all babbling to each other instead of talking to themselves and they are changing their clothes alot more even when they don't need to. Elliots have begun to look for men to go all the way with instead of doing mind sex to have baby Elliots. Now they are twisting their shapes to touch and join and it is kind of gross. And some of the Elliots are even being mean to each other. They need some laughter and I will play them some Eddie Murphy. The future is unknown captain.
Until it is time to be, Elliot.

Later the same day sigma 2 dear Elliot, I feel very sick about bad things on Elliottown and very bad about bad things here. Elliots are not laughing because I am not laughing and they don't cry because I don't cry over spilt milk and all that stuff. They are talking to each other and nobody will talk to me but I don't mind. They are doing sex things because they listened to me and Amelia talking about it because the guys in the cabin were talking about it. They wanted Dave to give them another lesson. I didn't tell them how I saw him with the drama lady. But I will die if the Elliots die. It is too many stresses for them. Our not being able to be and the sudden weirdness of INVISIBLE ELLIOT and new friend tribbles and having to lose them. I have been walking in circles all day but not on the softball field and I pretend that they don't say things but they do and I know it. Tomorrow I have to go hiking but I want to wear my sneakers instead of my boots. It is not good for us Elliots to hike. We need things to be in order and in place and we don't like going to new places and not knowing how to get home. I am packing a bag for the day hike with Evelyn, your letters, my ceramic tiles for the buried treasure map, all my pens and paper and stamps, the Eddie Murphy tape and the book Charlie X. Just in case. Whenever it is time to be, I will right away, Benjamin.

Star date supplemental dear Benjamin, Many things are better now. I went to Elliottown again when it was dark and played the Eddie Murphy tape for all the Elliots and they were so busy laughing they forgot about their joining up. It turns out that INVISIBLE ELLIOT was visiting another planet to look at life forms and living habits and he thought he'd be back soon so he didn't bother to inform the Elliots but travel in spacetime took a long time for some reason and he was late. Things are more calm. The Elliots can't wait for you and me to be together.
Until it is time to do that, Elliot.

Dear Elliot, It is good that you have made things better on Elliottown. And it is funny that you used Eddie Murphy because I was telling his jokes on the day hike. But it is bad that they were doing sex things. They can think about it but not do it. Thinking is ok but not every act is ok. I feel much better knowing things are good and I am as anxious to be with you as they are for me to be with you.

Until it is time to do that, Benjamin.

On the day of tau 2 at a secret time of the Elliots this is an urgent message dear Elliot, I will be leaving here soon and can help solve the problems of Elliottown. I miss you and Antares and Sherman but I am having fun. The ceramics project is complete and will fool everybody. I snuck out last night to place the parts for people to find. Evelyn gave me some good ideas of where to put them, and your ideas helped alot too Elliot, and now everyone will think there's buried treasure in the brook. Has Antares been back to Elliottown? If you go again, you must straighten out the barter system. It has been changed to a new ratio—3 amino acids now equal 1 pulsar, instead of 4 amino acids to 1 pulsar, and the young Elliots are having trouble understanding this. And it makes trade with Sargon difficult, since they are on a 5 to 1 system and are bad at fast math. I am sure that Hannah is snooping too. She does not understand Elliots, and you should not speak to her. And do not let her see you move. There is another problem too with the employment camps. The old Elliots can't work so hard anymore and they are sitting down too much. The young Elliots are tired of doing extra work and they might have a revolt. This must not happen, or the food will not be made and the Elliots will go hungry, innocent Elliots who do not know about how food is even made. When you go to Elliottown, do whatever work is left there so that everyone can eat and so that no one gets angry anymore. If they are bored of hot dogs and spuds you can make them pizza bagels. Everyone who ate the pizza bagels I made loved them so you should practice making them like an expert. Here is a secret message telling you how. I love saying spuds. Want a spud, stud?

HOW TO MAKE PIZZA BAGELS Take 1 unit of double texture grain and put on top of it half a unit of red die and good smelling green flakes and lots of shreds and give it 180 milimoments of radio waves and serve hot.

Soon it will be time to be, Benjamin.

Greetings Captain Elliot. This time the day does not matter and this is for you to laugh to. DELIRIOUS. Kirk fucks anything that's green. Mama used to fling that shoe. Thwack. AAAGGGH! Norman, how would you like to fuck me up the ass? Remember when David Letterman put on all that velcro and jumped on a wall? And the one where he put on a suit with alka seltzer stuck all over it and he jumped into a tank of water and almost fizzed to death? Do you remember which star called him an asshole? Then there was the one you didn't see when he got attacked by this monkey in a dress. He throws his card at the window. CRASH! AAAGH it is the late night thrill cam! You know kids, ladies and gentlemen Mr. Paul Shafer. It was Cher. And the time when the dog drank milk out of the guy's mouth on stupid pet tricks. That was gross. He reminds me of Dave my counselor a little. Did Dave remind you of David Letterman? I don't mean because they have the same name. Dave my counselor is funny. He watched a TV show about Republicans on his day off. He told me everyone should have voted for George Bush. He will only drive an American car. He always stares at this one counselor of the female type and now she looks at him funny. I think he likes her. She's the one I saw him with that time. He's a jock and plays too much softball. Elliots do not like playing softball and we don't like swimming either. But we like to cook now and Dave taught me how. Have you made pizza bagels? I can also light fires and make hamburgers and cheeseburgers and hot dogs but I don't like them as much. Next summer we'll join cooking club instead of drama club. We already know how to do improvisations and imitations but we do not know how to cook everything. And I had an idea. If I cook lots of things that are bland and let them rot I can put the food near the pieces of the buried treasure map and leave another kind of trail. If they can't find the ceramic pieces they can smell their way to the next clue. What do you think. But I wish you were here to do these things with me because I miss you.

Until it is time to be, Benjamin.

Past all days eta 2, theta 2, iota 2, kappa 2, lambda 2, mu 2, nu 2, xi 2, omicron 2, pi 2, rho 2, sigma 2, and tau 2, therefore This is the day of upsilon 2 dear Benjamin, Now you know that it is a really bad thing to push people off bicycles and hit them in the face. It is a bad thing to do because they do not forgive you or forget about it even if you do and they just get back at you later. They gang up in big groups and they get back at you. And when they do mean things you can't tell Dave or Chris or the directors because you deserve to be gotten back at and it is your fault to begin with. And if you tell on them they will only get back at you more like they said they would. Now you have to suffer with a wet bed and wet shoes and clothes with mud all over them because you were gotten back and you deserved to be. And now you can't tell Dave when he tells you to put on clean clothes that you don't have anymore. You can tell him that you don't have anymore but you can't tell him why you don't have anymore and that means you have to lie to him. And if you lie to Dave and he catches you he will get really mad and it is scary to see Dave really mad. They might do more bad things to you. They might go through all your stuff or take my letters away from you and hide them. Or they might keep stealing your paper but you can always get more at the office so that's not a big deal but it is very mean. Or they might push you in the lake. No they won't do that because there is always a counselor at the lake and the counselor will see them and get them in trouble, so maybe you should hope they push you in the lake. But we hate to swim and the water is cold. Or they might just keep on making fun of you. But that is not so bad. People make fun of all Elliots because they are mean and stupid and they don't understand us. It's not so bad if nobody talks to you. Soon it will be time to be and you can talk to me, Elliot.

It is late and my light stick is deteriorating dear Elliot, Well I should just tell you. I kissed Amelia goodnight. Actually, Amelia kissed me but I kissed her back. It was messy. I saw one of the pretty oldest girls kissing someone and it looked like they were french kissing and Amelia must have seen them too. I was glad she wanted to try it. She was kind of dumb though because she did it right in front of my cabin. I'm also glad that nobody saw us because they'd say I can't kiss girls, I can only kiss Elliots. Please do not be mad or jealous Elliot. I figured it would be ok. Benjamin.

On the day of psi 2 dear Benjamin, Amelia is bouncy and pushy. It was weird when she kissed you goodnight. And you should see what it has done to the Elliots on Elliottown. They have gone kissing crazy. It looks like they are glued together. I can hear you laughing as you read this. That is good because laughing is good. It feels good to be laughing so if no one says anything that is funny you can think of something funny like Elliots going kissing crazy and you can laugh by yourself. Now Amelia calls you her boyfriend and she thinks you must sit with her at the campfire, but what if you want to sit alone. It looks like this fire will be really big and bright and it is too bad that Antares is not at camp with you to help the humans light the fire. She will probably want you to kiss her goodnight this time. Boy will the Elliots go nuts.

You will be very different when it is time to be, Elliot.

Pre sunrise on omega 2 dear Elliot, Boy what a day and night. Me and Amelia sat together at the campfire. Everybody looked and giggled but we didn't care. I walked her back to her cabin at the end of the campfire. She has it much worse than me. If the guys in my bunk like Peter and Mark saw us going kissing crazy they'd make alot of noise. But all of the girls in Amelia's bunk saw us and nobody said anything. So they really don't care at all or enough to look and that's much worse maybe, I don't know. But I have alot more important things to talk about now. I need to make a map in art so that there is a guide on how to find the buried treasure pieces. But the map must look old and worn out so I will have to cover it in dirt and stuff and use thick paper so it gets all crinkly. So now Amelia and I are going out. I am going to make us walkie talkies so we can communicate when we're at different activities and stuff like that.

Until it is time, Benjamin.

On the day of eta 3 dear Elliot, I did not get a letter from you yesterday and I was surprised because I figured you would write to celebrate the first day of the third set. But I was very busy yesterday anyway doing lots of things. I soldered most of the parts together on the walkie talkie kit. I went walking up and down the camp road like I always do but this time Amelia joined me for part of the way. She did alot of talking about her cutout dolls and favorite movie stars. I told her how to open up a peanut butter jar. Then she left to put on her favorite skirt and I kicked out some dirt for her to have a special secret path, and I watched part of a really bad softball game and I sat behind the backstop so it felt like sensurround and the balls were all coming to hit me in the face. We went to the art room and picked out some colors for the buried treasure map. Then at night we had a sing and it was too late by the end for a walk or a goodnight kiss so I went to bed. Evelyn has been going to Elliottown regularly and she said that everything is fine. She can't wait to meet you. And I can't wait to see you either because even though there I am busy and even though I am with Amelia I am still by myself all the time.
Until it is time to be, for me and you to be, Benjamin.

Gamma 3 dear Benjamin, It is time that you spent more time with yourself instead of all of your time with Amelia. Amelia talks too much about things which are boring like old movies and cutout dolls, and she does not know about Eddie Murphy and she doesn't laugh at it, but she does know about Star Trek and that is good. But it is time to do some good thinking and listening. It is time to do some circle walks. You should check out the soil to see if it is good enough for Elliottown, and you should go to the brook and sleep a little. Tell me what you see. Until it is time to be, Elliot.

Dear Elliot, here is how to open a peanut butter jar.

From a seated position with jar on table and hands at sides, lift left arm by raising shoulder and bending at elbow so that arm is at chest level. Extend arm forward until fingers touch jar. Open up fingers by stretching hand muscles and make opening a bit bigger than the circumference of the jar. Place fingers around jar and grasp tightly by bringing fingers in toward each other. Repeat procedures with right hand but position fingers over the top of the jar. Descend and clench hand over lid. Using all arm muscles, hold parts of jar tightly. Make sure the right hand is on the lid only, the left hand is on the jar only. Twist right wrist to right with fingers clenched until tension of lid releases. Decrease tension of right hand. Slide fingers on lid back to original position and repeat the preceding sequence two more times. On the final twist, do not release tension in fingers but lift lid off of jar, carry lid to table surface, descend whole arm until lid touches table, release fingers completely.

Dear Elliot, this is what I heard on delta 3.

Stuff on the softball field

Batter up.
This sucks.
Play to second base ok second base let's go.
All right go go go go.
Safe at first.

Listening to stuff in ceramics

It got all lopsided.
Is the stuff in the kiln ready?
Who has the green. I need the green. Hello. Who's got
the green? I need it.

Listening to stuff all around

Hi Peter what's up?
What are you going to do for choice?
Can we watch the softball game?
Drama crew rehearsal in the Main House.
What's tonight.
A sing.
Shit. I wanna have another dance. Do we have a dance
on Saturday?
I don't know. Ask Diana.

What time did you get to bed last night?

Late, I don't know, like 4:00.

Jesus.

I'm exhausted.

Were you with Dave?

Yeah. We hung out in the main house for a while but
then we took off.

Where'd you go, the theater?

No—it's weird to do it in the theater. I mean, I teach there and
like he wants to do it on stage and it's weird, I don't know. We
were up to the loft in the barn. Someone else tried to go when
we were already there and they shined a flashlight up in the
loft. It was kind of embarrassing.

Who did it?

I don't know.

You look tired.

I'm asleep, actually. We always say how tired we'll be the next
day but that doesn't stop us from doing it.

Is it really good?

Yeah, it's really nice, you know? It's really easy.

That's great.

He doesn't push me or anything and it's always even and if it
isn't it just doesn't matter, you know? And sometimes we don't
do anything and that's ok too. I mean, you'd think all he wants
to do is fuck, you know, but he doesn't mind if we don't and he
likes to talk. And when we do he stays up afterward.

What?

He stays up—I mean awake. He doesn't just pass out.

Jesus.

I usually fall asleep first.
Wanna play vollyball?
Ok.
We need more people.
Jenny, Wanna play vollyball?
Yeah.
Get some more people.
Vollyball is boring. I wanna play tetherball.
RULE SIDE STICK RULE SIDE STICK RULE SIDE STICK.
I want this side.
So you can watch Peter.
Shut up I am not.
Yeah right.

On the day of epsilon 3 dear Elliot, I had kind of a bad night with Amelia. We were french kissing and I told her that I didn't just want to fuck and that I'd let her go to sleep first and she didn't understand, but then our five minutes were up and Dave called me back to the cabin. She ran back to her cabin, so do you think that means we have broken up? She didn't dump me really but I think we broke up. That would be ok though because she is very bouncy and she doesn't shut up and she always wants to talk about movie stars. But she also likes to talk about Elliottown. Maybe INVISIBLE ELLIOT is trying to tell me something. Maybe I did a bad thing.

Until it is time to be, which it will be in 4 more days, Benjamin.

Zeta 3, countdown 4, 3, 2, 1 until it is time to be Dear
Benjamin, Antares, Sherman and me are planning to have a big
party for you when you get home. There will be lots of peanut
butter and pizza bagels and we will get to meet Evelyn and we
will read Star Trek books together and we will laugh silently at
Eddie Murphy jokes when it's late and the parental units have
gone to bed we will watch David Letterman and think about
Dave and miss Dave but we will laugh alot because laughing is
a good thing but we will be sad too. I was sad to leave camp
because I missed you but also because I miss camp and Dave
and sex things and planning the ceramics project and the gravel
behind the backstop and sings and great big campfires that
Antares would have had a kiniption about. And I miss Amelia
and will miss her more at home. Dave too. It will be bad to not
be sleeping in the light by the brook and to be sleeping alone
in a room but we will keep us company. We will watch the
election in November and miss Dave and we will transmit
Republican vibrations to the poll places. And we will watch
cartoons in the morning like Winnie the Pooh and miss Amelia
and her being so bouncy. We will also learn to play softball
when it gets warm so we can play it next summer. Lots and lots
of things to do at home. Three days only.
Elliot.

Eta 3 late at night dear Elliot, We had a big fair today and I
ran a pizza bagel booth! There were lots of games and food
and a massage parlor that I didn't go to and a music stand and
a make up booth where I got H.A.S. painted on my forehead so
you and Antares and Sherman could be here with me at least in
some way. Lots of people bought pizza bagels. Dave and I
spent all morning making them in the kitchen and we ate alot of
them too. There were go carts and a sponge toss and Peter got
a bucket of water dumped over his head and he was really
mad. And the counselor band played and they were really
good. Amelia didn't get a pizza bagel. And we didn't dance
at the dance. I guess we broke up. I didn't dance at all at the
dance except with myself and my H.A.S. forehead. The last
campfire will be very sad. I will think about all the things I
will miss. There are only 308 days Inbetween this summer
and next summer.

It is almost time to be. Benjamin

Dear Elliot, Everything here is very sad now and alot of humans are crying alot, especially the oldest kids and even some of the counselors, and me too a little but only inside. Just when I got over being homesick I have to get used to being campsick. It will be very good to see you but I don't want to go. Amelia has been nice to me even though we broke up she wants to write to us and I told her we'd write to her too. We had a long sing in the main house and they sang all of my favorite songs like Stew Ball and Jet Plane and so many people were crying you could hardly hear the singing with all the crying. I wasn't crying over spilt milk and stuff like that since there's nothing I can do about it. Elliottown is sick. The Elliots have been crying so hard they've lost their breath and their throats are too stuffy to eat. Even the thought of pizza bagels makes them want to throw up. When it is time to be, you and I will comfort them together. And we won't talk to Hannah or mommy or daddy because they don't know anything about anything. Nothing about Elliots or Elliottown or Evelyn or letters or pizza bagels or buried treasure maps or Star Trek or Eddie Murphy or Republicans and American cars or softball 700 or anything important. So we have nothing to talk about. But we do. You and me have got alot of catching up to do don't we. It is very late. Does anybody really know what time it is? I will be home later this day I can't believe it. The last campfire was so sad. Everybody got to throw something in that was important to them that they love alot. I threw in some fake money I made from selling pizza bagels at the fair and I wrote down some of my favorite Eddie Murphy jokes and threw in the pieces of paper, and I put in a piece of clay from ceramics and I drew a big red H and laid it on top of the fire. It feels like it should be raining outside like in a movie or something. All my limbs hurt and I can't eat anything. How can something which seemed so bad turn out to be the best thing in the world. Next time I won't push people and I'll be patient when they make fun of me. I'll go swimming and play softball like I'm supposed to. I'll even send Evelyn to my home. I'll even dig up the buried treasure map. Just so I can be with Amelia and Dave and the drama lady and watch the elections and ride in an American car and talk about movie stars over walkie talkies. All the people who smiled when they ate pizza bagels and laughed when they heard me do Eddie Murphy are crying. Something is very wrong with this. If camp is better than home, then home should happen for only two months and camp should happen for the other ten. It is not good to be alone for so many months out of one year. It is not healthy. Elliots die when they're alone for too long. But now I have a plan. In the winter when camp is closed all the Elliots will take a vacation from Elliottown and come to Onianta and keep it warm and ready for us next summer. Our next project will be to reverse camp time and home time. But I'm sure we won't be able to do that during this long home time coming up. It will be a social revolution and humans might not be ready for that like Elliots were. So all we can do is start our countdown. Tomorrow will be negative alpha 1—the first day of a new negative era. I can't wait to see you on this day today when it is time to be. I can even wait for a little bit more. But come post sundown things will be as they always have been, and we will greet each other silently and we will keep on doing the same things we always do. And we will talk to each other without making noise and we will listen to each other and hide all the smiling, and it will all be today because today it is time to be. Benjamin.

PART
THREE

On the day of the rebirth and the first day of death Dear Elliot.

So sad we have to write again. I hoped we'd be together. It was the one good thing about leaving Onianta. Now there are no good things.

This place might be a very bad thing indeed. INVISIBLE ELLIOT cannot hear my cries through these walls and outside of this building. I thought this would all be white but I guess I was wrong I guess. Sherbet colors all over the place. Evelyn would have loved them. She is not allowed to visit. You are not allowed to visit either. I am not allowed to go home. I would not have asked to be here if I knew these things.

I do get to read Star Trek. And it's on TV here at 6:00 but I'm not allowed to watch it during dinner so I don't eat. There is not a mirror in my room. There is sun and I can see stars at night and I think about you and Evelyn and INVISIBLE ELLIOT watching over them. And me. I am campsick. I am hungry. If I am good I will get to make pizza bagels in the toaster oven but not by myself. At least this way I don't have to get bar mitzvahed.

Here is a nurse. She just asked me why I am writing while she tried to give me my medicine. I just hid my notebook from her. They will not take it from me, you think they will? Medicine makes me tired and I don't want it. Elliots don't like medicine.

I just took it. I have to. They don't let me watch Star Trek if I don't. It's not so bad, Elliot. I can write good in the mornings.

You know that it may never be time to be again. But in case it might, Benjamin.

On the second day of death dear Elliot

Lots of video games which is good. Lots of peanut butter. No
soda and only a little chocolate. I get to read my books alot.
Lots of kids want to talk to me. They always want to at bad
times, like when I am writing to you or talking to INVISIBLE
ELLIOT. I have only one bunkmate. His name is Eric. He
screams a lot. He picks his toes until they bleed.

Dr Dysan wants to talk to me today. He is nice but very dumb.
He does not understand things like you do. I think I will not talk
to Dr. Dysan.

For it to ever be time to be, Benjamin.

On the third day of death Dear Benjamin,

All the Elliots are really INSANE and CRAZY. They are loons and they should be put in the loon's house too. The tips of their toefingers and armlegs are crumbling off. Their center sources of light are hot and red. They are chewing on their coats and dust covers. They are licking inside themselves to blood in their stuffing. They are producing baby Elliots faster than tribbles produce tribbles. Sometimes they touch the rims of diagonal toefingers and armlegs and make themselves THREE DIMENSIONAL! Some of them are touching top toe fingers to top toe fingers, bottom arm legs to bottom arms legs, and are turning themselves into double O's, cyllanders, figure eights, tubes like see through umbrella stands. Some of them are flapping and trying to fly away. Their babies are DEFORMED. They have tumors on their midstrips and are turning into M's. They have all four armlegs underneath their midstrips and are turning into upside down double U's. Or they have diagonal armlegs and a midstrip and are both X's and T's at the same time—like a multiple personality in a BODY! Oh why why why did you get yourself into this mess? Look at what you've done to Elliottown!

On the day of the second death, Elliot,

I am so sorry about Elliottown. I just feel so bad about it and I can't imagine all of the distorted Elliots invading the planet. Oh what have I done to the Elliots? If I am good will they be fine? Tell me what to do. See if INVISIBLE ELLIOT can come and visit me here. I will make him pizza bagels. Maybe I can't. I am not allowed to cook in the hospital, but I get to do alot of art. I am doing a series of paintings of worshipping INVISIBLE ELLIOT. Dr. Dysan does not understand them but I will tell him nothing. NOTHING! Oh Elliot. What do I do about Elliottown? I have no light sticks and no Evelyn and I cannot contact the planet. Why did I want to come here? I have to get out. I have to get to Elliottown.

Dear Benjamin.

You are not a scuMbag anymore. I FEel
   soRRy

          foR you.

THE hOspital is funNY and it SMELLs
like
       likorish. WHY DO you lIKe it there.
It is YUcky AND
       kids do FUNNY
stuff liKE SlurpiNG AnD Domanos.
CAN
I COMe visit yOu again. Home SUCKS.
Daddy Broke
my hAIR-DO jeSSe doll and I hate him.

you dont
have TO CALL me LEMON even tho IT Is
my name.

Love LEMON S. The One and Onely.

104

On the day of the third death dear Elliot

Today Dr. Dysan asked to see my notebook and I said no.
Good thing I had a feeling he would. Eric wants to see it too.
Maybe he will get to. They keep changing his sheets because
the bottom half gets all bloody. Dr. Dysan showed me one of my
paintings and asked me to explain it. It was one of the
INVISIBLE ELLIOT series and I told him no. I hate when he looks
so mad at me. But he just won't understand. I miss Dave. And
Amelia. She said she'd write me letters but she does not know I
am here. I don't miss school. I would have failed it. And I'm
glad to not be being bar mitzvahed and if I stay here through
my 13th birthday it will be too late. I should act crazy so I can
stay. But I have to get out before camp starts so I can go. I will
be thirteen in a hundred and thirty seven days and I will still be
thirteen during the summer. They better not make me get a bar
mitzvah instead of going to camp.

What is happening on Elliottown? No sex can be tolerated. But
the Elliots must be nice to the deformed baby Elliots because all
forms should be tolerated. It is not nice to make fun of people
that are different or strange right? Old Elliots must make a
special effort to talk to them and be nice and not be too nosy
but be interested too. Like you are about me and Evelyn, and I
am about you and Evelyn, and you and Evelyn are about me
right? My armlegs and toefingers are full of pins and needles. I
saved my Hershey's Kisses for a midnight snack. I will save one
for you and one for Evelyn too.

So that it will someday be time to be, Benjamin.

Many days of death later dear Elliot,

I feel like throwing up all the time. It is so hot in here worse than Elliottown in the wintertime. Is it hot at home? I am so tired here all the time and I never do anything. They want me to swim in the pool. At least the water isn't as cold as the Onianta lake was but it's still water all the same. I said I wouldn't swim. Then I get all these stupid questions like why and why not and how come and what's the matter.

But more important, how are the Elliots on Elliottown? Are the deformed Elliots ok? Is INVISIBLE ELLIOT mad at me alot? There are many things that deformed baby Elliots can do. For example, as long as they have one armleg they can make pizza bagels and write letters. The ones that form double U's can invent new methods of transportation like roly poly and wheel thrusts. The ones like X's can become shooting stars and fireworks. Then as T's they can hold signs for road directions. It is not so bad really. I am sorry I did this to them. You can be nice to Lemon.

Until it is time to be which must be a long time away from now, Benjamin.

September 20

Dear Benjamin,

   Just a quick note to tell you that we love you and miss you and
are always so proud of you. We are excited for when you will be
well and can come home and stay with us. Everybody gets sick
sometimes. Some people get sick in their stomachs or hurt their
knees. They get physically sick. Some people get sick in their
thoughts and feelings and they are mentally sick. It is not a bad
thing. Some form of sickness happens to everybody. You know how
Daddy has his ulcers and Grandma has her artificial hip and even
Hannah got the measles one time. You are no different from them.
And just like they all do, you have to take your medicine so that
you will get better. Medicine makes people well again. Medicine
cures sickness. Please, honey, keep on taking your medicine so you
can get better too.

   I love you and am proud of you and hope you are feeling better.

Hugs and kisses,

Mommy

On the first day of a slower and slower death as slow as if time was going backwards dear Elliot,

Did you tell Mom to write to me? That was a dumb letter. I know about medicine and being sick and getting well. I asked to go to the hospital so I could get well, didn't I? That's what hospitals are for and they told me I was sick so I thought I should go. Now they're acting like I don't know what I'm doing.

Benjamin

September 29

Dear Benjamin,

I hope you like the surprises in this package. I sent you nuts and dried apricots and chocolate raisins and some other surprises since you said you wanted a lot of sweet things. Sweet things for a sweet boy! There is also a letter for you sent to our house. I guess you didn't tell any of your friends your new address. The letter is at the bottom of this box.

See you on Saturday,

XXX and OOO

Mommy

Amelia Brenner
315 West 83rd Street
New York, New York 10024

Dear Benjamin,

How are you? I am fine. I saw The Wrath of Kahn last night and it was really good like you said it was. I ate a peanut butter sandwich while I watched it and I opened the jar very carefully. I miss camp a lot, don't you? I hate school. My hair got so long this summer! I can pull it down to my waist when I tilt my head. My mom got me this pad of paper for a coming home present. Do you like it? I like the lettering. I wish I could write in script that well. What are you doing? Was it good to see Elliot? Have you been to Elliottown? I know you hate when I ask you but I really want to know. Do you like school this year? Is Hebrew school really as bad as everyone says it is? I was wearing that turquoise skirt you liked today. I hope you can come to New York or else I can go to Connecticut so we can visit. I'm bored. All day I think about going to bed. I'm sorry about all the messes at camp.

Yours very truly,
Amelia

In the beginning phase of reverse death in super slow motion dear Elliot,

Lots of funnytalking all around here. All grown ups talk funny like there are no kids around.

Slurp slurp.

Nononononononono.

I get off at 6:00.

Do you want to.

No dessert in 310.

Melinda's out.

6:00. You can get me off anytime.

Did you read Amelia's letter? It was nice, but she is a human and even though she thinks she knows all about Elliots and Elliottown there is much she does not know and I will never tell her. Weirdo to ask about it right?

Have you been on Elliottown? Why are you not writing? How does Elliottown seem? The Elliots must be more mello because I am very mello, like mello yellow which I hate a lot but Dave loved even more than he loved Jolt Cola and Peter 1. I wonder if Dave got a bar mitzvah. I think he must have dumped the drama lady. He must be a sportsfucker. Mutherfucker

mutherfucker mutherfucker mutherfucker mutherFUCKING MARK!

Write soon to prolong this dying. Why are you not writing or answering me? Until it is time to be, Benjamin.

On the day of ART and MUSIC death dear Elliot,

I do alot of art and music. But no Eddie Murphy music. I made this painting in the INVISIBLE ELLIOT series where INVISIBLE ELLIOT is a black spot and all these diagonal lines in perspective grow out of him and go off the paper. The lines are thick and colored in with lime green and peach like all those sherbert walls. I'm playing the zylophone in the drum group. There are these long ropes hanging from the ceiling which I get to climb up and slide down like a fireman. Eric has to wear socks when he sleeps now. And he has to wear them taped on to his hands too. I talk to Dr. Dysan Mondays and Wednesdays and Fridays but I don't say much. He asks me alot of stupid questions like do I miss you Elliot and then he watches me do my art and practice my Eddie Murphy. Why do I like Eddie Murphy so much. Because he's a funny mutherfucker. Why do I watch Star Trek instead of eating and don't I know they won't let me watch it if I don't eat? Because I like it. Why else? I don't know. Because I like it. It's my favorite TV show. Isn't that a good enough reason? How was my visit with my mom and my sister? Fine. Can you tell me about it? No. Did they seem nervous? No, different. Was I anxious? Do I get anxious alot? What makes me anxious? So I broke into my favorite David Letterman routine and pressed my face real close to him like he does to the camera, but Dr. Dysan kept asking those stupid MUTHERFUCKING questions and he wasn't laughing. Do you think he has no sense of humor Elliot? Maybe he doesn't understand about laughing. If he doesn't understand about laughing soon, I will never tell him the secrets of Elliottown.

Until it is time to be sometime, Benjamin.

October 12

Dear Benjamin,

My my, you must have a lot of super friends to keep writing to you like this. This one came the day before yesterday—looks like it's from Onianta! Daddy and I got your camp reports and they were just glowing and wonderful. What wonderful memories you are sure to have from this place. Maybe someday you can grow up and go back and be a counselor, just like your counselors Dan and Chris, right? We will be thinking of fun new things to do for next summer, won't we. Let's hope that we can.

Hannah can't wait for baseball season and all of her clothes have lemons on them. Most of them are yellow to begin with. Grandma and Grandpa giggled. We want to see you very very soon so keep on taking your medicine and getting well so we can have a picnic. If the doctors will let you bring him, maybe your roommate can come too.

Hugs and Kisses, sweetie,

Mommy

Onianta

ANNUAL LETTER TO ALUMNI

Our Annual Onianta Reunion will be held on January 22 at 12:00 at:

Billy's Beefy Burgers
804 Broadway
New York City

We hope you can plan to come. There are always lots of people you know there. It's great fun. Make a day of it. Arrange a spree with your cabin after lunch. We'll have audio and video tapes of last summer available on sale.

We'll write letters to campers who are unable to attend. Be sure to drop us a note if you won't be able to make it and we'll read it aloud.

Report on the 1994 season:

Well, we had a lot of rain for a while, but by mid July the sun poked out its face, warmed the lake, dried the grass, and restless bodies played hard in the hot, wonderful weather. Our wonderful nurse had practically nothing to do—oh, a few sore throats here and there, but nothing major—just the way we want it to be!

Onianta does its best to keep up with changing times. The TV studio has been up and running for a while now, and the chef has perfected his alternative vegetarian menu, including zucchini boats, bean and cheese burritos and tabouli. Stained glass and jewelry projects were just beautiful—a small lampshade and a lovely silver bell were among the many wonderful projects exhibited at the crafts show. As always, there were dozens of beautiful ceramic vases and leather bracelets. The canoe overnighter faced twenty portages and leeches and soggy sandwiches. We held our second Triathlon and our first Mountain Bike trip, and we played a new all-camp game called New Hampshirian Gladiators, complete with costumes and make up and dozens of events. We had a terrific rock band, four cabin plays and an outstanding full-length musical. We were proud once again to not distribute NRA Riflery Awards.

All in all, it was one of those GREAT summers, absolutely unique. New groups of campers and staff bring new ideas and passions, and one summer is always different than the rest. We hope to continue to work with such terrific kids, and we look forward to seeing ALL OF YOU in January.

At the shred of light toward the rebirth dear Elliot,

A reunion! I am sooooo excited. I hope we can go, or at least I can go. Would you be mad if I went without you? Do you think I'll be out of here by January? I can if I want to be. Since I wanted to be here to begin with then I can leave when I want to, to end with. I get to see Amelia and Dave and Chris and the drama lady and it will even be good to see Mark the mutherfucker. And we'll watch the camp video and listen to tapes from old sings and maybe they'll have pictures of the stream so I can see my marks for the buried treasure and know it is still there my secret. To return to next summer when I get to go back to Onianta and play and watch softball and make ceramic disks and treasure maps and brand-new Elliots! And I get to see Dave again and I can ask him if he had a bar mitzvah and maybe he can tell me how he did it so maybe I can do it too.

Please write back Elliot. You have been very lame about your letter writing. You must get off with the nurse anytime or something.

Until the half life of timing to being, the half life in the fourth week of January at the start of the new Star Trek moon, Benjamin.

Elliot,

I told Dr. Dysan that I want to leave in time for the reunion. He said we'll see. I said I asked to come in and now I am asking to get out. He said it isn't that simple. So what does that mean. He said am I ready for school. I said maybe I could go to the reunion and then come back. Then he said I have to write a letter to a human for every letter I write to you. I guess that if I do that dumb thing I will get to go.

He did not say I had to write one for every letter you write to me.

SO START WRITING!

Dear Dave,

How are you? I am fine. How is school? Is college really hard?
Do you see camp people at all? Like who? Do you get to see
Diana and Chris and people like that or do you guys all live far
away? Do you miss camp alot? I miss camp alot. I can't wait
until the reunion. Are you going to go? I am. Definitely.

I am not in school now because I'm sick for a little while. I will
go to school again after the reunion. I got a letter from Amelia
and the camp newsletter but that is about all. How is school for
you? I will start again after the reunion. I wish I could go to your
school. It would be so neat if camp time was really school time
and school time was really camp time so everything was all
backward so we'd have ten months with camp and only two
months with school. School sucks but I miss it. I will go back
after the reunion. I wonder if I'm on the camp video at all.
Are you?

Please write if you can. See you soon.

Sincerely,
Benjamin Sherman

Dear Benjamin,

I did not like your MUTHERFUCKING drawing of me.

Elliot

Dear Elliot,

I feel like I have been sleeping for weeks and days and centuries. I am feeling very upset about your letter and I do not know what to do about it. I thought it was a good drawing with lots of secret symbols. Diagonal lines off the page for the everlasting, and also for INVISIBLE ELLIOT, soft colors for friendship, center point for Elliottown. What's the matter? I feel like I am thirsty all the time but water doesn't work. I'm sorry so please don't be mad at me.

Your friend, Benjamin

Dear Lemon,

Dr. Dysan is making me write this letter to you. You were right
not to like him when you met him. You would like my roommate
because he picks his toenails even more and grosser than you
pick your armleg fingertoe tips. There's gonna be a new Beatles
group, I heard. I think yellow is a wonderful color and that sour
things are good. But not with cream or milk. Don't cry over spilt
milk. Come visit some more. Maybe Starfruit is a good name for
you to have later. They have origamy here too.

Love, Benjamin

Dear Benjamin,

I was wondering why it is that you do not want to talk to me. I would like to get to know you better, but it is hard when you won't talk to me at all. Maybe we could make some pizza bagels together. Would Wednesday be all right with you? Also, I was wondering if, since you are such a terrific letter writer, maybe you could write a letter to me? You can tell me what you think about pizza bagels in the letter.

Your friend,

Lawrence Dysan

October 30

Hey Benjamin—

  How's it going, dude? You must be psyched to be
out of school for a while. I am pretty sick of school
myself, let me tell you. But school is a good thing to
do in the end, so get better soon so you can get back
there, ok?

  I heard from Peter 1 and he's cool. He says he got a
buzz cut. Some of the guys on staff came to stay for
a weekend and we had a good time. I keep up with
Chris and Diana a little and that's pretty much it.

  I miss camp too, but I don't know if I'll be back
next summer or not. I might have to take some
classes here, maybe get a part-time job, we'll see.
But I'm into this reunion thing, so hopefully I'll see
you there.

Thanks for writing.

See you—

Dave

On the day of peanut-butter sticky tongues, on the diving board edge of death, dear Elliot, that's what it feels like. Like peanut butter stuck to the roof of your mouth, only I haven't been eating any peanut butter but my mouth feels all sticky and gooy. They told me it's normal. I said if it's so normal why don't you just give me some peanut butter to make it right. No snacking. For dinner? Will you turn off Star Trek? Will you let me stay up until 11:30 so I can watch Dave Letterman? Will you talk to Dr. Dysan in the morning? Will he stop being a MUTHERFUCKER at me. No Benjamin, no peanut butter for you.

Dear Amelia,

How are you. I am fine. Elliot is fine too. She says hi. I am very far away from Elliottown right now. I am in this place so I can get better so I can go back to camp next year, that's why I asked to come to a place like this but everyone thought it was pretty strange but good. It's kind of like a hospital but they don't like to call it that. Some of it is pretty and the yard smells like Onianta during a campfire right after the rain. Actually Elliot and I aren't getting along too well. She's gotten so moody. Maybe you could come see me here. They let my sister in so they do let in girls, just not Elliots. Thanks for writing me a letter.

Sincerely,
Benjamin Sherman

Stop talking about armlegs Benjamin.

No you can't have any peanut butter even though you want
sweet things all the time, and obviously Dr. Dyson will not stop
being a youknowwhater because you tell the nurse to tell him to.
At least you don't look so dumb because you're tired all the time
anymore, like the time you almost fell over backwards what a
dope! The Elliots have been thinking about making a Star Trek
movie starring themselves, because you know that all the guys
on Star Trek are fake and even though there is a space the final
frontier there is no voyage of the starship Enterprise. Don't you
listen?

Wouldn't it be something if Elliottown caught a speed of light
ray and got farther and farther away, like Dr. Dyson said it
might, and since they don't have any dilithium crystals they can't
get to warp 8 and counterthrust? Elliot

November 17

Hello sweetie,

We were so happy to see you last week, and we think we all had a very productive meeting with Dr. Dysan. Hannah really likes him now because he said it was fine for her to play with her Hair-do Jesse doll. I can already tell how much The Michaels Center is helping you. And I am glad that you don't have as much trouble going to the bathroom with this new medicine.

Sweetie, I hope that you will be all better by January too, but we just can't make those kinds of promises right now. There are reunions every year—that's why they call it a reunion. I hope you will be able to go to it too. And Elliot.

Jelly beans, Benjamin? I never knew you liked jelly beans. Or rock candy. I will send you a little of each, as much as the center will allow, so you can have them on Sundays.

Lots and lots of kisses and hugs and love,

Mommy

Death is forever so nobody really knows what time it is dear
Elliot.

Pizza bagels with Dysanhead are not the same. The kitchen
here smells like plastic space suits and not butter and cookies
like the Onianta kitchen. I hid one under the oven for you to
have. Do you think things are different or maybe that's just me? I
don't know. I understand if it is time for Elliottown to meet
another galaxy just so that you can go there and still not leave
mine. I guess it was dumb to push Mark the mutherfucker off his
bike. When I grow up I think I want to be a buried treasure
maker. Or an Elliot.

Dear Mommy,

Dr. Dysan said I had to write to you so I am. How are you? I am ok. I finished all the candy you sent me so could you please send me some more. Dr. Dysan said that if you come with Daddy next time we can make pizza bagels. I am sure Lemon will be extra careful not to spill the milk. Please take good care of my friend Elliot.

Sincerely,
Benjamin

Benjamin,

You are a freak. Elliottown is ready to put on its jet propellars and zoom into the year three thousand. So that way you will be dead before we meet up with earth time again. We are all sick of this stuff and we don't like watching over hospitals anymore. Get better or we will take off.

Elliot

Dear Elliot,

Are you trying to kill me? This is the closest to dead I have ever been. Why have you gotten so moody and mean? Please stop because I don't like it very much at all. I feel sort of funny from it, like crying, but us Elliots have no tears. We have lots of throwup. When I read your last letter all over again that was how it made me feel. I am sorry if I have done anything to make you mad. Please don't call me a mutherfucker anymore because I am always very kind to you.

Love, Benjamin

November 26

Dear Benjamin,

Please don't hang up the phone on Mommy anymore. It really hurts Mommy's feelings when you do that. But I know you are upset so I understand so we can just pretend that it never even happened.

I got a wonderful letter from you when you were feeling so much better. It made Daddy and me so happy that you wrote us a letter. Maybe you could write us another letter, sweetie?

If you do get out of bed and take a bath, I will be so happy that I will send you a whole pound of Jelly Bellies, the kind you like with extra watermelon ones, ok? Hannah said she would use some of her allowance to get you peanut butter cups too. We want so much to visit at the end of December but we want to see you doing your best.

Happy Turkey!

We love you,

Mommy and Daddy

Stein, Sherman, Wharton and Daniels
Investment Banking

Jeffrey Sherman

1751 Main Street
Suite 400
Middletown, Connecticut 06457
Tel: (203) 554-4000
Fax: (203) 554-4323

November 27, 1994

Dr. Lawrence Dysan
241 Central Park West
New York, New York 10024

Dear Dr. Dysan:

Peggy and I have appreciated all of your efforts with our son
Benjamin, but permit me to come right to the point. Frankly,
with all due respect, The Michaels Center does not seem to be
working for Benjamin. Although he did show some signs of
improvement in weeks past, and granted he seems more even-
tempered than he was reported to be at camp, he seems to be
slipping significantly. No doubt his minimal overall progress
is due to the strength of the medication you have prescribed.
Certainly when he is no longer medicated he will be back in
fantasy-land and unruly.

Benjamin hung up the telephone on us the other day. He was
uncharacteristically rude and ill-mannered throughout the
entire conversation. As I listened on the extension, my wife

became more and more gentle, while Benjamin grew more and more snide. This may seem like a small adolescent gesture to you, perhaps just a "bad mood," but it was tremendously upsetting to my wife, it was inexcusably out of line, and it made us quite skeptical about this so-called healing process. Disturbances do not allow for unrestrained abhorrent behavior. No doubt you are an expert in your field. Perhaps the simple fact is that Benjamin is not suited for psychiatric treatment and was simply born different.

We would like to meet with you and discuss the situation further if need be. Please call my secretary to arrange a mutually convenient time.

Thank you.

Jeffrey Sherman

JS/kj

Dear Ms. Elliot,

I am writing to you on behalf of Benjamin Sherman. He is very upset that you were mean to him in your letter and now he will not get out of bed. Could you please apologize to him? It would make him feel a whole lot better. You do not have to give him any reasons, he said. He just wants you to be his friend again.

Thank you,

Lawrence Dysan

GET up yOu old EXSCUMBAG

I WAnt tO pLAy WIth YOU so
HEre is Some

CANDY
bye.

Dear Dysanhead,

You can tell the mutherfucker that I might be sorry if I get to eat
some Reeses peanut butter cups.

Elliot

Amelia Brenner
315 West 83rd Street
New York, New York 10024

Dear Benjamin,

I was so so glad to get your letter.

I have been reading the most wonderful books. I take them with me everywhere. It is great to read books when you are sick that's what my mom says so maybe you should read some books. She says it is wonderful. I am sorry you are sick. Get better by the reunion or else!!!!!!

Love Amelia

On the everlasting invisible void of nonlife. What did I do that was so bad Elliot? Are you ashamed that I am in a hospital or mad that I didn't bring you? You know that I was not allowed to bring you and that the only thing that I am doing here is trying to get out and fake it for them so that we can be together. So that if they think that I don't love you anymore they will stop bothering me. But now you are sounding like Mark and all the guys from Hebrew school and regular school who are so mean. Did you find another human who is better than me? Now I am not hungry for anything even pizza bagels and I stretch out my arms and legs away from my body on the bed so that I look like an H with a head on it. Does Evelyn love someone else too? Did I do all of this for nothing at all? I am sorry if I was a bad human and if I had tears I would show them to you.

Love, Benjamin.

Dear Dr. Dysan,

Here is the letter you want from me. If I make it a nice letter then maybe you could do something to help Elliot. Maybe something is really wrong with her to make her so mean and cranky to me because Elliot has never been mean and cranky to me before and I don't think I really did a bad thing so I think there must be something really wrong with her. And you are a doctor of thoughts and feelings so maybe you could make her thoughts and feelings better. Please. I swear I'll be good and nice to my mother and Lemon and I'll keep writing letters to humans and maybe you are right that Elliot should stay home on my bed when I go to school and stuff so I promise I will try that for as long as I can stand it. What's wrong with Elliot? Thank you.

Sincerely, your friend Benjamin

Dear Amelia,

Everything is really bad. Elliottown is a mess. I wish you could
help me. How are you? I am fine. Not so good. I am dying to
go to the reunion are you going to go? Everything is a real big
mess. Kind of like my old friend's toes after he picked them.
Kind of like the armleg fingertoe tips on Elliottown. I better see
you there. I wish you could help me. Write back soon.

Sincerely,

Benjamin

Dear Ms. Elliot,

Your friend Benjamin is very upset. We were wondering if you
might be able to meet with us on Friday. There are a few things
we need to discuss. No need to respond. Just be sure to arrive
on Friday at 1:00. Thank you.

Dr. Lawrence Dysan

LAWRENCE S. DYSAN, M.D.
241 CENTRAL PARK WEST
NEW YORK, NEW YORK 10024
(212) 934-2424

December 8, 1994

Mr. and Mrs. Jeffrey Sherman
118 Church Street
Middletown, Connecticut 06457

Dear Mr. and Mrs. Sherman:

I appreciate and sympathize with the concerns expressed in
your letter. Part of the inherent frustration in my field is the
slow pace of recovery in all patients. We all wish for instant
cures. Unfortunately, as in most serious diseases of the body,
psychological and emotional healing takes a great deal of time,
just as one must spend a period of time recovering after a surgi-
cal procedure or feel the ill effects of chemotherapy or endure
terrifically painful therapy after a slipped disc. Benjamin is certainly coming along quite nicely. In fact, I have been rather
pleased with his progress. I feel that it would be irreversibly
damaging to remove him from The Michaels Center at this
stage of his treatment, and I cannot recommend or support this
course of action at this time.

We are clearly on the verge of an important and potentially successful breakthrough with Benjamin. As we discussed on the
phone, the time has come to bring Benjamin's stuffed letter to
the hospital for a visit. Would you be kind enough to bring it to

the visitor's information desk by noon on Friday, December 23? As always, I will present you with a full report on Benjamin's progress as it occurs.

Thank you,

Lawrence S. Dysan

One the second day of the eternal void, the ultimate death of all deaths my old friend Elliot

Maybe this should be my last letter to you since you have been so awful to me. Maybe you are just a crankhead for some reason that I don't know. I know that Dr. Dysan asked you to come and visit me and I hope you do and I hope you are not so mean anymore. I didn't do anything wrong and if I did I am sorry and will you just please forgive me. I have been told that all the Elliots are about to die too. They are gasping. They are going to hold their breath in case Elliottown catches a speed of light ray and zooms into the future of the year a million. I will not be able to be there with you all because I am here and I don't think The Michaels Center will let me out to catch a speed of light ray and fly off with the planet Elliottown into the year a million. Besides I'm a boy.

But I am excited to see you anyway. Maybe we can get on the outside of the void together.

See you soon. Benjamin

Day four of the void dear Elliot

I guess it is a bad sign that you are not writing back to me anymore. Dr. Dysan said it is a good sign, but we never trust anything that Dysanhead says right? That it is time for you to go now. Good means bad like you always said to me right?

Day seven of the void dear Elliot

I have a feeling I know what will happen when you come to
visit me and it is the worst thing of all that could happen. You
know what the worst thing is that you could do to me and it is
what you will do to me I am sure. You won't talk to me right?
No more secret Elliottown language during the session. I'll try to
talk to you in silence and you will say nothing back. And you
know what that means right? It means that Elliottown caught that
speed of light ray and soared off past my earth lifetime without
me. It means you will be a body without a soul anymore right?
Not that you mean to be mean but that you are gone.

Please don't catch the speed of light ray and go away from me.

Elliot.

Friendships change you know, He said. That people get
different and people change and sometimes move away and
that all people die. So is that what you are doing? Growing up
without me he said. I am scared to see you on Friday. Maybe
you should not come.

So you are still coming today Elliot. Bet you won't talk to me. I made them make me take my medicine this morning. Elliots don't like medicine and we don't cry over spilt milk cause we have no tears. We love Dave Letterman and counselor Dave and DELERIOUS and when Cher called him an asshole and the green lady that got off anytime with Kirk. Tholian's Web and the drama lady and Amelia. Maybe I shouldn't have told her anything. Is that what did it Elliot? And peanut butter and jelly bellies our new friend and most of all PIZZA BAGELS!!!! Pulsars and 3 to 1 ratios and amino acids and Sargon. Maybe INVISIBLE ELLIOT was bad all along and just fooled me. Like all you were was make believe. Evelyn went away a long time ago I guess. I liked all that company. Now when they find the buried treasure map we will not be around to tell them what it was. You should take my light stick with you when you go cause you will need it more than me.

What if the speed of light ray lets you off in the dark? Then you won't be able to write me more letters. They won't ever get to me anyway cause by the time they get to earth time I will be a different changed moved dead friend.

Benjamin.

Woosh.

Zoom

ZZZZZZOOOOOOOOOOOOOOOOOMMMMMMMMMM!!!!!!!!!!

Bye.

LAWRENCE S. DYSAN, M.D.
241 CENTRAL PARK WEST
NEW YORK, NEW YORK 10024
(212) 934-2424

January 9, 1995

Mr. and Mrs. Jeffrey Sherman
118 Church Street
Middletown, Connecticut 06457

Dear Mr. and Mrs. Sherman:

I hope you had a wonderful holiday, and it was a pleasure to see you with Benjamin on Christmas Day. Do not be disturbed by his quiet acquiescence. As if he were mourning a death, the healing from loss is slow. Lethargy, lack of attention span, listlessness, are a common and a normal part of the process. There is no such thing as an instant-recovery pill—they are all time-released.

That notwithstanding, it will soon be time to release Benjamin from The Michaels Center, to send him back to his familiar surroundings, his family, his school. . . . He is aware of this. Reentry may be difficult; in fact, it may involve some regression on his part. It will be crucial to monitor closely his behavioral changes. You can expect him to be moody and withdrawn, perhaps hyper at odd hours. Again, let me stress that all of this is normal for a period of time. Only you can observe the frequency and severity of these mood swings. Let us try to reassimilate him for at least six weeks. As always, I will be available to answer any questions or concerns you may have.

I am reducing, not removing, his medication. The dosage will change from two pills a day to two on one day, one the next, always after breakfast and alternatively after lunch. If he is feeling well, Benjamin may be reluctant to take his medicine. It is critical that he continue, however, so we may gradually wean him off the drug, if indeed that is possible, and let me state for the record that I suspect it will not be for some time.

I also suggest that you remove Elliot from Benjamin's closet. Do not get rid of the toy—make it less inviting.

We should arrange a meeting in order to answer any questions and clear up any confusions you may have. As always, Friday afternoons are fairly open for me. Please call my secretary at the hospital to schedule a conference.

Sincerely,

Lawrence S. Dysan, M.D.

January 14, 1995

Dear Harold and Lucy,

Again, we would like to thank you for all of your personalized attention to Benjamin this summer—and what a wonderful season he had at Onianta. Jeffrey and I greatly appreciated your patience with our son.

Benjamin's return home from camp was not so smooth, unfortunately. It became necessary to hospitalize him just a few days after his arrival. We think, though, that the intensive psychiatric treatment and those miraculous new medications have helped him tremendously, and he is scheduled to leave the hospital on February 1.

It is a shame that his release will occur after the reunion and he will not be able to attend. Perhaps it is a blessing in disguise—who knows what an onslaught of summer memories would do to his well-being.

I am sure the party will be lovely, filled with fun and games. Have a wonderful time, and thank you again for all of your attentiveness.

Warmly,

Peggy Sherman

Yay Sweetie!

We can't wait for you to come home!

There will be lots of yummy food and presents. Pizza and jelly beans and rock candy and peanut butter. You can have a slumber party with all your friends in a few weeks if you like. And since school just started a few weeks ago you will not have too much to make up. We will help you whenever you need help. We are so proud and happy that you got well.

1,000,000 kisses and hugs,

Love,

Mommy

DEAR BENJAMIN,

CONGRATULATIONS!!!

WE ARE ALL SO PROUD OF YOU!!!

WE'LL MISS YOU, BUT WE'RE GLAD

YOU'RE ON YOUR WAY.

-THE STAFF

IT will BE Good when YOU are
HOME.

I WILL BE nice to YOu since YOU
dont hAve anY More letters any more.
I maDE YOU oragamy in the Closit

I didnt LIKE IT like an ONLY child like I
NEVER had a bROTher

YOU can call me LEMON or
HANNAH
both are ok now for you to call me.

Dear Benjamin,

I thought you might like to leave The Michaels Center with a different sort of letter.

You know, now, that Elliot is safely stored away in a part of the old you. It is good to remember her and Evelyn and Elliottown and know that the part of you they live in is appropriately moving farther and farther away.

You will meet people with many of Elliot's special qualities—warm and affectionate and trustworthy and fun. They will be even more real, and they are better company, and they will care about how you feel and what you want. Everybody is scared of new people. The secret behind the mystery is that not all new people are so scary after all.

I know that Lemon can't wait to see you, and your mother is so proud. I'm sure Amelia and Dave and the Restons will be glad to know you're home, feeling well.

So it may feel strange sleeping in your old room. And you might miss The Michaels Center like you might miss Elliot. But you will feel a bit better when there's less medicine to take, and soon you will be involved in plans and projects you can't even imagine right now. And if things start to feel overwhelming or out of control, if you feel yourself slipping (you know the warning signs), you can always call me. Or write. I promise, I will always write back.

Warmly,

Lawrence Dysan

To whom it may concern.

Speed of light rays do strange things. I think they are friendly
but sometimes they are not but maybe they know better I don't
know. Yes they are friendly I have decided. Everyone should
get to meet one if I can bring them here. Who is that now me
or you or you or me.

And all the stuff gets smaller in the woosh away. We are
moving backwards and forwards all at one spacetime. Like
being sucked in at the middle with our armleg fingertoetips
flying behind and in front. What happens to the throwup
when everything moves so fast. Pssssssstt. Zoom. I wonder
if it feels scary I think. There is no time for lonesomeness I
guess. Soaring on a speed of light ray away from home to
home. Fun to fly I bet.

Yes. All smaller and wooshing and fun to fly. Nothing to be
scared of and no time for lonesomeness. The further away
and back ahead we go. It will be all nice and dark. Speed
of light rays know where to go. You are lucky if you can catch
one like me.

Natio

Do you knov
information
National Me
tion and loc
and organiz
emotional p
and treatmer

Contact us t
you can help

Natio